N
NORTH BRANCH

W9-AYF-846
3 1192 01196 2188

The Offer

Other Five Star Titles
by Robert J. Randisi:

Delvecchio's Brooklyn

The Offer

A Novel of Suspense

Robert J. Randisi

Five Star • Waterville, Maine

This novel is a work of fiction. Names, characters, places and incidents are either the product of the author's imagination, or, if real, used fictitiously.

First Edition
First Printing: January 2003

Published in 2003 in conjunction with Tekno Books and Ed Gorman.

Set in 11 pt. Plantin by Ramona A. Watson.

Printed in the United States on permanent paper.

Library of Congress Cataloging-in-Publication Data

Randisi, Robert J.
The offer : a novel of suspense / by Robert J. Randisi.
p. cm.—(Five Star first edition mystery series)
ISBN 0-7862-4865-3 (hc : alk. paper)
1. Police—Missouri—Saint Louis—Fiction. 2. Saint Louis (Mo.)—Fiction. 3. Stalking victims—Fiction. I. Title. II. Series.
PS3568.A53 O35 2003
813′.54—dc21 2002190703

The Offer

PROLOGUE

The tattoo artist, whose name was Ned—jeans, Doc Martens and a sleeveless T-shirt revealing flesh almost completely covered with tattoos—was regarding Amy Wheaton's perfect butt the way an artist studies a blank canvas. He'd just asked how far down she wanted her tattoo to go.

"That's an interesting question," Amy said. She had her head turned to the left to speak to Ned and now turned it to the right toward her husband. "What do you think, Sweetie?"

Vince stepped forward and Ned looked up at him expectantly.

"Look here," the artist explained. "The rose itself will rest right in the dimple, but the stem will disappear *into* her butt cleavage so it looks like the rose is growing out—"

"I get it," Vince said.

"I need to know how far to go with the stem." Ned stood back to await their decision.

Amy was not a large woman, and she had a body that was almost devoid of fat. Taut breasts, slender hips, smooth creamy skin and the neatest, tightest behind you ever saw. Vince felt his breath coming faster, as it always did when he looked at his wife.

"I want thorns," Amy said. "Don't forget the thorns."

"I can do thorns."

"Vince, honey?" Amy said.

"It's your ass, babe," Vince said.

He smiled as Amy craned her neck to look at him. She

knew him better than anyone ever had or ever would. In those four words she could hear his excitement.

"But what do you think?"

"I think it would be sexy as hell."

"Damn right," Ned said.

"Let's go for it," Amy said.

"It's done."

Ned stood up and stared down at his handiwork.

"How does it look, Vince?"

"Baby," Vince said, sincerely, "it's a work of art—just like you."

"Is it red?" she asked.

"Blood red," Vince said.

"And it's got thorns?"

"They look so real I don't know how they're not pricking your skin," Vince told her.

"Can I see?" she asked, craning her neck.

"Relax," Ned said. He moved a mirror that was suspended above her on a metal arm, tilting it so she could have a look. "See?"

"Oh, wow!" she said, impressed. "Ned, you *are* an artist."

"It's true," Ned said. He scratched his gray, scraggly beard which was itching from all the sweat that had flowed into it during the job. "I gotta go wash up, kids. It's been real."

"Plastic okay?" Vince asked.

"Fine."

Vince handed over his Amex card and Ned went to prepare the bill.

"It's beautiful, Vince," Amy said, still admiring the artwork in the mirror. "Thanks for letting me get it."

"Letting you?" he asked. "I told you, it's your body."

“No, baby,” she said, her voice a sexy purr, “it’s yours—all yours when we get home.”

He put his hand on her gently, careful not to touch the tattoo, which *had* to be sore, and said, “I can’t wait!”

Later Amy lay beside him in their bed, her head on his shoulder, his arm around her. She was lying on her side because her rear end was still sore.

“That was great,” she said.

“Better than great.”

“But . . .”

He looked down at her.

“But what?”

She looked up at him and said, “I think it’s time to make the offer, don’t you?”

“Let’s not go too fast,” he said, after a moment. “After all, we don’t want to frighten this one away.”

She sighed and said, “You’re right. I’m just . . . impatient.”

“Well,” he said, “that’s why I’m here. I’m the patient one.”

“I know,” she said, snuggling up against him, “you keep me in check, don’t you?”

“We’re a team,” he said, “we keep each other in check.”

“We are a good team, aren’t we?”

“Uh-huh.”

She closed her eyes and, just before drifting off to sleep, she said, “I just hope nothing bad happens . . . like last time.”

ONE

Jack Jones stared across the desk at Doctor Fabian. What a name. Fabian. And the doctor didn't look anything like the 50's singer. Jones had orders to report to the shrink—first, it had been once a week, then every two weeks, and now it was once a month.

"Still playing sex games?" Fabian asked.

"Sure."

"And enjoying them?"

"Yep."

"And you still don't see anything wrong with them?"

"Nope."

Fabian's pen tapped on the desk, something that used to annoy Jones. However, once he decided that Fabian was doing it on purpose it suddenly didn't annoy him, anymore.

What still annoyed him, though, was Fabian's superior attitude. It wasn't because Jones had been battling depression for a couple of years, and it wasn't because of the three partners he'd lost. It was because of Katy, and the fact that she was a stripper—and young.

He wondered if his being married to a stripper would have been such an issue if Fabian was a man.

The psychiatrist stopped tapping her pen and ran her hand over her hair; to be sure it was still in place. She was a handsome woman in her forties, her blonde hair still worn long rather than cut short like most middle-aged women. Jones could never understand that practice. He was amazed women didn't know that cutting their hair short when they reached a certain age just made them seem older. At least, to him.

Fabian opened Jones' file folder and made a show of looking it over. She raised her eyebrows when she did this, and pursed her lips in what Jones thought was a very un-doctor like but feminine gesture. Jones liked that, because there were times when he could easily forget the doctor was a woman. He liked a reminder every once in a while, like a swish of nylon from beneath her desk to remind him of how long and attractive her legs were.

"Why don't we do a recap here, Detective?"

"Fine."

Fabian lowered her file and looked at Jones.

"Do you intend to answer all my questions with one word?"

Jones smiled and said, "Or less."

Fabian sighed. Another very feminine gesture, the long suffering sigh.

"It was two years ago that your partner of five years, Teddy Lenders, was killed in a shootout on the street."

Jones invoked his "or less" remark and remained silent.

"You were there, and managed to kill the, uh, perp. You were subsequently investigated, as it was felt by some that you might have actually, uh, executed the man on the spot."

"Exonerated," Jones said.

"Yes," Fabian said, "well . . . seven months later your new partner, a woman named Leslie Daniels, was also shot and killed in the line of duty." The doctor looked at Jones over the top of the folder. "You were training her at the time."

"Yes."

"The, uh, perp is in prison at this time, serving a life sentence."

"Right."

"You didn't kill that one." She didn't ask it as a question, but was stating a fact.

"No."

"Learned your lesson, hmm?"

No answer.

"Then ten months ago your third partner, a man named Ralph Mollica—after working with you for only a few months—took his own life," Fabian looked at Jones again. "That was rather traumatic for you, for reasons we have gone into before."

Many times before, Jones thought, and closed his eyes . . .

This was his third dead partner in sixteen months.

That is, if this one was dead, but he had a real bad feeling.

Not that they were great friends or anything, but they were partners.

"Find that sonofabitch and drag him to work!" his Boss had ordered. "And he'd better have a good goddamned reason for why he's been missing for three days . . . like he's dead."

It was supposed to be a joke, but it wasn't a joke to him, not after losing two partners so close together.

As he tried the doorknob he couldn't shake the bad feeling he had. The house just seemed too still. In fact, his partner had been telling him that ever since his wife had left with the two kids—after asking for a divorce—the house had seemed too quiet, too damned still.

He circled the house, tried the other two doors, found them locked, as well. He went to the garage and looked in the window. The car was there, and it wasn't running. At least that was something.

Okay, so now he felt justified in breaking in, all he had to do was choose which door looked the easiest to pop. He picked the kitchen door. He put his shoulder against it, exerted some pressure and the lock popped like a doll house door. Cop's house, he thought, crappy lock. Go figure.

He walked in and the smell hit him right away. Jesus . . . his vision started to blur and he felt the tears roll down his face. Jesus, not again . . .

He paused in the hall, used the heels of his hands to try to clear his eyes. Out of habit he removed his gun from his holster as he started moving again. The house was all on one floor and while he had never been there his partner had talked about his home life enough over the last three months that he knew the layout. To the left would be the den the man used as his refuge, straight back and to the right the bedrooms.

He knew he'd find him in either the den or the master bedroom.

It was the den.

He was seated at the desk. He must have settled his left cheek against the desk top and then put the gun in his mouth and pulled the trigger. Didn't want to fall out of the chair. The gun was there in the right hand, trapped in a death grip. The top of the desk was soaked with blood.

He holstered his own gun, started to reach for the phone but his right hand was shaking. He tried to stop it with the left, but that one was shaking, too. Then his legs went and suddenly he was on the floor, his back against the desk, hugging himself. His whole body was shaking, his eyes were streaming, and he couldn't help but think, "Not again, not another one . . ."

Three in sixteen months.

He'd wait for the tears to go away and the shakes to stop before he called it in. After all, the dead man wasn't going anywhere . . .

"We determined," Fabian droned, as if speaking to a child, "that since you didn't even know him that well, the incident was a reminder that you yourself had once thought about doing the same thing, oh, more than two years ago."

Jones scratched his eyebrow and looked away.

"That was back when your depression first started," Fabian went on. "You told no one about that, though . . . except me." The woman seemed smug. In point of fact, she had browbeat the admission out of Jones, which had not endeared her to the detective.

"After the death of your third partner you met and married your wife, the former Katy Foucet . . . um, who is a, uh, stripper."

Fabian always said "uh" before she uttered a word she thought to be beneath her, such as "perp" or "stripper." Jones actually liked the habit, as it pointed out what a tight ass the woman was.

"Now, some of your colleagues," Fabian went on, "as well as myself, consider your marriage to a stripper half your age to be a result of the trauma and depression you've suffered."

"That's their problem—and yours," Jones said.

"You, however," she went on, ignoring the comment, "have said on many occasions that she has kept you sane, and has quite possibly saved your life."

Fabian set the file down.

"Which is where we are now," she said. "Detective, you realize that when this marriage fails—and it will, it *has* to—it might just be the final straw that drives you over the edge."

Jones didn't answer.

"You *must* realize," Fabian went on, "that unless it is *you* who calls an end to the relationship it will be *devastating* to you."

"That's not going to happen!" Jones snapped, and immediately became angry.

Fabian sat back and looked satisfied with herself. She'd managed to pull more than one word out of Jones, and she considered that to be a triumph.

"I have to go to work," Jones said, standing up. He'd lost this time, and he hated both himself and Fabian for it. He wasn't going to ask her to call his C.O. At this point that would be a major point loss, and he was too many points behind, as it was.

"Same day and time next month, then, Detective?" Fabian asked. "Hmm?"

She penciled in the appointment on her calendar even though Jones left without confirming it.

TWO

Earlier in the day Detective Jack Jones had entered the office of his boss, Captain Phillips.

"Got a minute, Cap?"

"Just about one," the man said, sourly.

Jones actually hated going into the C.O.'s office because he usually came out of it smelling like cigar smoke. But before leaving the house that morning he'd promised Katy he'd talk to him . . .

"I'm not one of those wives who pushes her husband, Jack," she'd said over breakfast, "but you deserve better than this. Don't you agree?"

"There was a time I wouldn't have," he said, taking her hand, "but being with you has changed all that."

She lifted his hand to her lips and said, "Then do it, baby—not for me, but for you."

"I've got to go see Dr. Fabian first," he said, "but when I get to the office I'll do it . . . I'll do it for both of us."

"What is it, Jack?" Phillips asked, breaking into Jones' thoughts.

"I need something to do, Cap."

"Do your job."

"These days my job consists of clerical work," Jones complained. "I'm not a clerical man, Cap, I'm a detective. I need to get back into the rotation."

Phillips passed a hand across his forehead wearily.

"You were a good detective for a very long time, Jack," he said. "Lately . . ."

"Lately nothing, Cap," Jones said. "My problems are behind me. I'm ready to start catching cases again."

"You still seeing the department shrink?"

Now it was Jones' turn to respond sourly.

"Yeah. In fact, I just saw her this morning."

"See what she says," Phillips suggested. "If she thinks you're ready to catch some cases have her call me."

Fat chance of that, Jones thought.

"I think I'm ready, Joe," Jones said, using the Captain's first name. They'd known each other a long time, but Jones rarely used his superior's first name.

Phillips frowned. "All right, Jack. Let me think about it. Maybe something will come up, something I can use to ease you back in slowly . . ."

"Okay, Cap," Jones said, moving towards the door. "That's all I ask. Give it some thought. Thanks."

"Sure, Jack," Phillips said, "sure."

THREE

Robin Lobianco parked in the spot marked Assistant Curator, which was okay since that was her job at the St. Louis Art Museum. Located in sprawling Forest Park the position at the Art Museum had been one she'd been seeking for a long time and, one short year ago, she'd gotten it. Of course, a lot of other things had happened during that year. For one, she and her husband, Frank, had recently separated. Also, she'd made new friends with a couple who had turned out to be—well, strangely interesting. Her friendship with the Wheatons was just one of many bones of contention between her and Frank. He'd been against becoming friends with them, which, of course, in the midst of their marital problems, was reason enough for her to pursue the friendship. Lately, however, she was beginning to think that—on *that* subject, anyway—Frank may have been right.

She was afraid that she had made a grave error just three nights ago when—after a dinner that included a couple of bottles of wine—she had allowed the young couple to entice her back to their apartment, where the three of them proceeded to go to bed together.

Now, three days later, she was still embarrassed by the whole incident even though there were some parts of it that were enjoyable.

She hurried up the steps and into the museum and made her way to her small office. She did not want to run into her boss because she was several minutes late—again. She had been elated when she had been accepted for this job last year, but had never expected so much to happen in her life to keep her from concentrating fully on it.

She closed the door and sat behind her desk, not concentrating on her job even now. Instead, she was thinking back three nights, feeling both foolish and adventurous for what she had done.

She had always been very satisfied with her body, and her husband—and other men—had always made her feel desirable. However, being naked in the same room with Amy Wheaton, who hadn't an ounce of body fat on her, had made her feel like a cow.

Vince Wheaton, however, had made her feel that she was the most beautiful woman in the room—and she knew that wasn't true. Amy's face was classically beautiful, while Robin knew that hers was a collection of seemingly mismatched parts when, put together, made her attractive, sometimes even sexy, but never beautiful.

Being with Vince had excited her, but having Amy there had made her self-conscious. And when Amy said, "Just relax, darling, and enjoy it," she had done just the opposite. She had tensed up, especially when Amy touched her.

"You have marvelous breasts," the other woman had told her, touching them. "I wish I had breasts like this."

That had surprised her. Amy Wheaton seemed so self-assured all the time, not only comfortable with her body but extremely so.

"Doesn't she have lovely breasts, Vince?" Amy had asked her husband?

"Exquisite," Vince had said, and then he began to pay special attention to them while his wife watched.

Okay, having this astonishingly handsome young man—probably not yet thirty and several years her junior—make love to her while his beautiful wife watched *had* been a turn on. Even now, alone in her office, she could feel herself flushing. There was even a touch of shame involved, because as soon as Vince Wheaton's perfect penis had entered her she'd had an orgasm. It had taken her and her husband a couple of years to get to the point where she would achieve orgasm during their lovemaking. She didn't know what it was. Vince's penis wasn't *that* much larger than Frank's. Maybe it had just been the situation itself.

After her first orgasm, though, there had been more, as Vince cupped her buttocks in his hands and moved in her and Amy lay beside them, talking to her, touching her . . .

The phone rang at that moment and she jumped guiltily and stared at it. She had been avoiding the couple for three days. What if this was one of them? At this time of the morning, though, it was more than likely her boss calling to complain about something. In an odd turn of events her superior, William Dance, had been hired after she had been, so he'd had no input into hiring her. She suspected that was the reason that they had not been getting along since he began his job one month after her.

She didn't want to talk to either of the Wheatons and she didn't want to speak to her boss, but she answered the phone. It was none of the above.

"Hello?"

"Robin?"

She immediately recognized the voice of her husband, Frank Lobianco.

"Frank," she said, surprised. "Why are you up this early?"

"I've been trying to get you for days," he complained. "What's wrong with your machine?"

After the night she'd spent with the Wheatons she had

disconnected her answering machine until she could decide how best to handle the situation.

"The damn thing is on the fritz," she lied. "I haven't had time to get it fixed. Why have you been calling me?"

"Why?" he asked, belligerence plain in his tone. "Because I'm your husband, that's why."

"Frank," she said, with a sigh, "you know what I mean . . ."

"Okay, okay," he said, "sorry." When called on it Frank's belligerence always turned into a little boy pout. Neither worked really well with her, anymore.

"What can I do for you?" she asked, then quickly added, "I don't have much time . . ."

"Have dinner with me?"

"When?"

"Tonight."

Not tonight, she thought. *God, she'd be too embarrassed* . . . she had to resolve this thing with Vince and Amy before she could face Frank again. Why had she even allowed herself . . .

"Tomorrow night, then," Frank said.

"Frank . . . I'll have to call you."

"Robin," he said, seriously, "we have to talk."

"I agree, Frank," she said. "We do have to talk, but this week is bad. The new show is coming in and I have to supervise the placing of all the pieces—"

"All right, all right," he said, surrendering. "Today's Wednesday. Can we do it Monday?"

She started to say she didn't know, but then relented and said, "Okay, let's do it Monday."

"Good," he said, relieved, "we can go to our—"

"Let's talk over the weekend to arrange where and when, all right?" she said, cutting him off before he suggested "their" place. "I have to run. Dance is on my ass."

He chuckled. The phrase had become a joke with them when Dance had first started working there.

"All right," Frank said. "I'll talk to you on the weekend, sweetheart."

"Thanks for understanding, Frank."

"I always understand, Robin."

"Right," she said, and hung up. That was a big part of their problem, right there, she thought. He actually thought he "always" understood when, in fact, he "never" did.

When the phone rang again several minutes later she felt sure it was Dance and answered it.

"Hello."

"Robin."

Her heart started to beat faster and she got a queasy feeling in the pit of her stomach.

It wasn't William Dance, it was Vince Wheaton.

FOUR

She had first met Vince and Amy Wheaton at a fundraiser that was held at the Art Museum. It was six months ago, just about the time the problems with Frank were really starting to get bad. They'd started the morning off by making love, which had left Robin something less than satisfied, so that she was edgy when the party rolled around.

She had taken her black dress with her to work so that she could change there before the party and not have to go home. Wearing that meant also wearing her black bra and panties, and while changing in her office—with the door locked, of course—she had paused while she was naked to reflect on that morning . . .

Frank had awakened her by rolling to her side of the bed and kissing her neck. That didn't happen very often, so she was pleased. She rolled onto her back to kiss him and things started going quite well.

She reached between them, delved into his underwear and found him hard and ready. She tugged on him, stroked him and freed him from the confines of his jockeys. Suddenly, she rolled over onto him, causing his hand to fall away from her. She straddled him and tugged his underwear down, tossing it away, then got rid of her nightgown and panties.

"I want you in me," she said, and mounted him . . .

Later they'd had *the fight*.

He'd bitched because she had taken the play away from

him when she removed his underwear and mounted him. They'd had this "discussion" before, about how she got too aggressive when she got very excited. She tried to take control, and that was "his" job—or so he thought.

The upshot of it was he had gotten up and gone into the bathroom, and she had been left less than satisfied. How many men complained that their women were too eager, too rough, sometimes? Didn't most men like that? He'd taken back control, hadn't he? But then all he'd done with it was flip her onto her back, poke into her and jackhammer her until he was satisfied.

She had slipped on her SBD—Simple Black Dress—and examined herself in the full-length mirror she'd put in her office during her second week on the job. She was wearing the scoop-necked black dress, not the high-necked one. This one showed the slopes of her breasts, while the other one fit her more tightly and often showed off her large nipples. Dance had complained more about the high-necked one than the scoop-necked one, but then he had a problem keeping his eyes off her breasts, anyway, which she thought was one of their major problems. She didn't like the way he stared at her, and he was embarrassed and angered by his inability to keep his eyes off her. He was, after all, a married man, and he was married to a woman who thought that "looking" and "cheating" were the same thing. She had him trained—to feel guilty about looking, not to stop.

She'd checked her hose to make sure there wasn't a run, then slipped into her black pumps. She'd decided not to wear the Fuck-Me's. That would have sent Dance over the edge, completely.

Finally satisfied with her appearance she left her office and went to play hostess at the party where she'd first met the Wheatons.

★ ★ ★ ★ ★

When she first saw Vince Wheaton the impact of his amazing good looks was immediate—aided, largely, by the fact that she was . . . well, in heat. She walked over to him to play good hostess and introduce herself. He saw her coming and watched her in a very frank, appraising way that made her itch. She wanted to reach down and rub her crotch but she didn't dare. Maybe, she thought, she could get him to do it later . . . but that was just a dirty, naughty thought. In four years of marriage to Frank she had never cheated on him—and had never felt so ready to do so as she did at this moment.

"Hello," she said, when she reached him, "I'm Robin Lobianco."

"Ah," he said, "the lady whose name was on the invitation."

"I invited you?"

"You did."

She smiled what she hoped was a sexy, flirtatious smile and said, "How smart of me."

At that point he put out his arm to encompass the woman next to him and said, "You invited us."

"Us?" Robin's heart sank.

"Yes," he said, "I'm Vincent Wheaton and this is Amy Wheaton."

Robin looked at Amy and couldn't believe how gorgeous she was. The lavender dress she was wearing was obviously a size two and Robin immediately felt about as sexy as a cow. The woman had perfect little tits, like hard peaches beneath the dress, an impossibly tiny waist and, Robin knew, when she turned around she'd have the tightest, most wonderful butt, the type that women spend hours a week at health clubs trying to cultivate. Robin had always felt that her own butt was just a little too big, but right at that moment she felt as if she were lugging around a sack of potatoes, back there.

"Hello," Amy said, giving Robin a dazzling smile and extending her hand, "what a wonderful party."

Robin accepted the hand and said, "Thank you."

"May I get you ladies a drink?" Vince asked.

"Oh, yes, darling," Amy said, "I'd love a white wine, if they have it."

"We do," Robin said. "We have a full service bar."

"Your doing?" Vince asked.

"Yes."

"You're a smart woman," he said. "People dig into their wallets much more willingly when they're liquored up. A drink, Robin?"

"I'll have a white wine as well, thank you, Mr. Wheaton."

"No, no," he said, "call me Vince, or no white wine for you."

"All right, Vince, thank you."

"Be back in a jif."

As he walked away from them Robin couldn't help but look at his butt. The man was impossibly good-looking, as gorgeous as his wife.

"He's a dish, isn't he?" Amy asked.

Robin flushed, caught looking.

"It's okay," Amy said, putting her hand on Robin's arm, "you can look. Most women do."

"I'm sorry—"

"Don't be," Amy said, laughing. "He's just divine."

"Well," Robin said, "I'm sure the men look at you just as much as the women look at him."

"Do you think so?" Amy asked. Her expression seemed completely disingenuous.

"Well, of course," Robin said, "you're beautiful."

"Thank you, Robin," Amy said, seeming pleased, "but can I tell you a secret?"

"Sure," Robin said, wondering why this woman would want to confide in her.

"I'm trying to get Vince to buy me a set of breasts like yours."

Robin felt a flash of anger that the woman would think she was packing silicone in her bra.

"These are not—"

"Oh, no," Amy said, quickly, "no, no, I didn't mean to imply—well, they're beautiful, and naturally so and since I can't have them naturally I just . . . well, I'm sorry, I didn't mean to offend you. I just . . . envy you."

Robin felt her eyes go wide. These two were just about the most beautiful couple she'd ever seen, and they had to have money to have been invited to the fundraiser, and Amy envied her?

"You know something?" Amy asked, as Vince walked towards them with the drinks.

"What?" Robin asked, helpless against his looks and the confidence of his walk and unable *not* to watch him.

"I think we're going to be great friends," Amy said.

FIVE

They did become friends, in spite of—or because of—the fact that Frank took an instant dislike to them.

"There's something wrong about them," he told Robin, after meeting them for the first time at a restaurant. "Something shady . . . they're too slick."

Robin assumed Frank was jealous of Vince's looks and thought that maybe he was even attracted to Amy. After she and Frank separated two months ago her friendship with the couple accelerated. They were very supportive of her after the break up, and called her to have dinner often. Initially she felt like a third wheel, but they were so easy to be with that the feeling soon faded.

And then, three nights ago, the sex happened. Now she was sitting at her desk with the phone in her hand, panicking . . .

"Robin?" Vince said, yanking her back to the present. "Are you there?"

"Uh—"

"Listen, dear," he said, his tone so solicitous, "Amy and I are concerned about what happened. We don't want it to ruin our friendship. I know this must be very awkward."

"Well . . . yes, it is . . ." Robin stammered. "I don't know what I was thinking, Vince . . ."

"But I want you to know that we don't regret it," he went on. "You have become very precious to us."

"Uh, that's sweet, Vince, really but . . . I can't talk right now. I have, uh, work . . ."

"I understand," he said. "Why don't we have dinner tonight or tomorrow?"

"Vince, I can't—"

"Amy and I want to clear the air, Robin," he said, "please." He sounded so desperate. If it were just him, she thought, and Amy wasn't involved . . . but that was silly.

"Vince—"

"Just dinner," Vince said, "so we can talk. Really, we can talk about anything together, you, Amy and I. We feel that close to you."

"Vince—"

"Meet us at Duff's," he said, "at seven. If you don't show up—well, we'll be devastated . . . but we'll try to understand."

"I don't know . . ."

"Please?"

She put her hand to her forehead and shook her head, but she said, "All right."

"Wonderful!" he said. "We'll see you there, sweetheart."

Sweetheart, she thought, as she hung up. He called her that so effortlessly and even in front of his wife it had never seemed out of line. Now it just felt . . . wrong. She also marveled at how easily he had persuaded her to have dinner with them when her own husband had not been able to sway her into saying yes to him.

Vince Wheaton was an amazing and gorgeous man. If not for the fact that she was married to Frank, and he was married to Amy . . . but what was she talking about? Hadn't she already slept with him, even though she was married? It was the first time she had ever cheated on Frank—but was it cheating if they were separated?

The phone rang again, startling her. She'd already spoken to Frank and to Vince, so what could be worse? She only had to pick up the phone to find out.

It was her boss, William Dance, and he wanted to see her in his office right away.

"We're having some problems, Mrs. Lobianco," Dance said to her.

"What kind of problems, Mr. Dance?" she asked. "With the new displays—"

"With that, yes," Dance said, "but mainly I'm talking about you."

"Me?" *What's the problem?* she thought. *That you can't keep your beady little eyes off my tits?* Even now he was staring at them through his thick-lensed glasses. His eyes always looked watery behind his glasses, and he had the most awful taste in ties. He also suffered from a terrible case of dandruff and—when she got close enough to notice, which wasn't often—he had bad breath. She was always surprised that he had managed to remain married to the same woman for thirty years.

"What problems have you had with me?"

"Lateness, for one thing," he said. "You have been coming in late almost every day for the past few weeks."

"Well . . ." she said, but she couldn't mount a defense that wouldn't make her sound pitiful. She was newly separated from her husband, handling herself things they used to handle together. She was keeping later hours than she used to, because Frank had always insisted they be in early. And she had just recently participated in her very first *ménage à trois* with a very beautiful couple and was feeling terribly guilty about it.

What else?

"Well, I'll try to make sure that stops," she said.

"And you've become somewhat absentminded, it seems."

"Absentminded? About what—"

"There was a staff meeting earlier today. Did you forget?"

God, she had forgotten!

"Yes, sir, I did, but—"

"It's the third such meeting you've forgotten this month."

"That's not exactly true, sir. There was one I hadn't forgotten about, but simply couldn't make . . . but I see your point."

"I hope you do," he said. "Your contract is coming up for review very soon, Mrs. Lobianco."

"Yes, sir."

"I'm simply making you aware . . ." he said.

"Yes, sir," she said. "I appreciate it."

"That's all. You can get back to work now."

"Thank you, sir."

She turned and walked to the door, knowing full well that he was watching her ass. She tried to walk a very straight line to the door, but Frank and other men—Vince Wheaton included—had often complimented her on her walk and how unconsciously sexy it was. Now that she was very self-conscious and felt as if she couldn't walk at all.

SIX

"Why don't you file a sexual harassment suit against him?" Brenda Telford asked her at lunch.

"Hmm? Who?"

"Dance," Brenda said, "your boss, that's who. Who have we been talking about?"

Brenda was Robin's closest girlfriend. They were the same age—thirty-one—and that was where the similarities ended. Brenda had never been married and enjoyed playing the field. She never saw the same man two months in a row. She was tall, blonde, willowy, and men flocked to her. Robin attracted men but was not the "eye candy" that Brenda was. They had met five years ago when they both worked in the same art gallery, but since that time Brenda had never worked in a gallery again, while Robin had moved up the ladder to her present position. Brenda played the field as much with jobs as she did with men.

"You know," Brenda said, "your boss is right about one thing."

"What's that?"

"You have been pretty absentminded lately."

"Have I?" Even her reply was said absently.

"You've got a lot on your mind, girl," Brenda said, "and it's time you shared with your buddy, Bren."

They were sitting at a table in a section of Forest Park that was away from the Art Gallery. Robin didn't want anyone from the gallery coming across them and interrupting them. That was because she had actually been thinking about sharing with Brenda, but she wasn't exactly ready yet.

"You need coaxing?" Brenda asked. "Who tells you everything about her life?"

"You do."

"Who doesn't keep any secrets from you?"

"You don't."

"Who's the best friend you ever—"

"All right, all right, Bren," Robin said. "Just gimme a minute."

Brenda put her egg salad sandwich down in the wax paper she was using as a plate and leaned forward. Robin had long ago ignored her tuna salad.

"Oh, this is juicy, isn't it?" she insisted. "That's why you haven't been able to tell me."

"Bren," Robin said, "could I ever tell you something that would make you think badly of me?"

"Never!"

"How do you know?"

"Because I love you, Robin," Brenda said. "We're friends. If you told me you were sleeping with my guy I wouldn't—well, that's a bad example. I never keep a guy around long enough. Is this about Frank?"

"No."

"Did you find out he was cheating?"

"No," she said, "Frank wouldn't cheat anymore than—" Robin stopped short when she realized what she had been about to say.

"Anymore than what?" Brenda asked, and then her eyes lit up. "Anymore than you would?"

Robin looked away.

"Oh my God," Brenda said, grabbing Robin's arm, "this is so cool. You did, didn't you? You slept with somebody?"

"Brenda," Robin said, "you cannot repeat this to a soul. Do you understand? Not a soul!"

"I won't, I swear," Brenda said, raising her right hand. "Now give. Who was it?"

"Well . . . you know that couple I've been telling you about? The Wheatons."

"Oh," Brenda said, excitedly, "that beautiful man you said makes Pierce Brosnan look like Quasimodo? The one Frank just hates?"

"Vince Wheaton."

"Ohmygod!" Brenda said, fanning herself with her hands. "Ooh, God, you slept with him?"

"Well . . ."

"Come on, Robin! You're killing me. Is he a good kisser?" She lowered her voice. "Was he big? Oh God, did you take him . . . did he put it in your—"

"It wasn't . . . just with him."

"Oh, you slut!" Brenda said, after a moment of stunned silence. "Did you do it with two men at once? Who was the other one? Does he have a brother?"

"It . . . wasn't two men."

Brenda put her hand over her mouth and squealed like a kid on Christmas morning.

"You had a ménage with a man and a . . . woman?" she asked, in a hushed tone. "Oh, God, you're my new hero."

Robin blushed and nodded.

"Oh *God,* girl," Brenda said, digging her nails into Robin's arm, "you have to tell me everything."

"Brenda," Robin said, "I'm embarrassed by it. I can't—"

"You can't stop now," Brenda said. "You brought it up, so you must want to talk about it."

"Well . . . it has been bothering me . . ."

"Bothering you?" Brenda asked. "Robin, you finally did

something adventurous and it bothers you?"

"But I never should have done it." Robin lowered her voice and looked around to satisfy herself that no one was near enough to them to hear them.

"Why not?"

"I don't like women . . . that way," Robin said.

"Oh, so what," Brenda said. "So you did it once, big deal."

"Have you ever done it?"

"A ménage?" Brenda replied.

"Yes."

"Of course."

"With another woman?"

"No, but . . ."

"But what?" Robin asked.

Brenda looked around now, giving herself the same satisfaction that no one was within earshot.

"I'm only telling you this because you told me yours," Brenda said. "You have to swear never to tell a soul."

"I swear."

Brenda hesitated, then said, "I . . . have been with women . . . before."

"Bren!"

"It was in college," Brenda said, "and I was just experimenting."

"Not since?"

"No," Brenda said, "I don't like women that way, either . . . but my God, Robin, you were with him! Wasn't he just gorgeous?"

Robin flushed again and said, "Oh my God, he was . . ."

"And was he big? Bigger than Frank?"

"He was . . . bigger than most, I guess . . . and he's got a real pretty—but I was always aware that his wife was . . .

you know, right there. I didn't really feel right . . . you know, doing anything to him."

"Did you do stuff with her?"

"It was more like . . . she did it to me, you know? I wasn't really . . . into her."

"But was she into you?"

"I think so," Robin said. "It was funny . . . I mean, Vince was really good and all . . ."

"How good?" Brenda asked, leaning forward.

Robin also leaned in and said, "Real good," and both women giggled.

"But what?" Brenda asked.

"But when they were . . . you know, doing it with each other . . . that's when they *really* got into it. I mean, Bren, this couple is crazy about each other."

"Then why invite you into their bed? It was their bed, wasn't it?"

"Oh, yes," Robin said, "we went back to their place . . . but I don't even remember who invited who . . ."

"Oh, Robin," Brenda said, "take my word for it. It wasn't your idea." Suddenly, Brenda grew serious. "You don't think they . . . slipped something into your drink, do you? That date rape drug, what's it called?"

"No, no," Robin said, "I don't believe that. I mean, I was drunk, not drugged and, well . . . I did it."

"You have a point," Brenda said. "I didn't know you had it in you."

"I don't *want* it in me," Robin said. "I mean . . . don't want to do it again."

"With him? Or with both of them?"

"Well, I certainly don't want to do it with her . . ."

"But what if he asked you again? Alone? Just the two of you?"

Robin bit her lip and said, "I'd be tempted."

"Maybe . . . if he's interested," Brenda said, slyly, "you could invite me next time."

"You bitch."

"Slut."

They laughed then and began to gather up the remnants of their lunch. Robin had to get back to work, and Brenda had to go home and get ready for a date.

"We're not finished talking about this, you know," Brenda said as they walked to their cars together.

"Oh, I know," Robin said. "I have to talk about this, Bren. I don't know what to do."

"When did this happen?"

"Three nights ago."

"Three nights?" Brenda said. "And you're just telling me now?"

"It's not an easy thing to talk about," Robin said, "even with you."

"Have you seen them since?"

"No."

"Are you going to see them again?" Brenda was breathless with anticipation.

"He called me this morning."

"Mister Gorgeous?"

"Uh-huh."

"What did he want?" If Brenda was any more excited she'd be hyperventilating.

"They want to have dinner with me to talk this out."

"Both of them?"

"Yes."

"Maybe they're just as embarrassed as you are."

"I don't think they're embarrassed, at all," Robin said. "He told me they didn't regret it."

"Oh, I just thought of something."

"What?"

"What are you going to tell Frank?"

Robin almost recoiled from the question.

"Why should I tell Frank anything?"

"He's still your husband, Robin."

"I know that, Bren."

They reached their cars and stopped.

"Frank called me this morning, too," Robin said.

"About what?"

"He wants to have dinner and talk."

"What did you tell him?"

"That I was busy and I'd call him."

"And what did you tell Mister Perfect?" Brenda asked.

"That I'd meet them tomorrow night . . . maybe."

"Robin . . . let's look at this logically. Where's the harm, really? You've never cheated on Frank before, have you?"

"Of course not!"

"And you're separated, so this isn't really cheating . . . is it? I've never been married, so I don't know the rules."

"I've never been separated before," Robin said, "so I don't know them, either."

"So what are you going to tell the perfect couple at dinner?"

"That this won't ever happen again," Robin said.

"Will you stay friends with them?"

Robin hesitated, then said, "I don't know. I really like both of them . . . as friends, you know?"

"And if Mister Wonderful wants a little more on the side without the Mrs.?"

"He won't—"

"But if he did?"

Robin bit her lip again and said nothing.

SEVEN

Robin made it to work on time and managed to get through the early part of the day without any casualties. She felt sure that once she had cleared the air with the Wheatons, and then with Frank, she'd be able to concentrate on her job—and her life—and things would start going a lot more smoothly.

However, as the clock moved closer to 3 p.m. and the end of her workday was only two hours away she started to get more and more nervous about meeting with Vince and Amy. When the phone rang at 2:45 she nearly jumped out of her skin, but she answered it. Maybe it was them, postponing the dinner until another time.

When she answered it, though, it was Brenda, calling to offer moral support.

"Are you still going to meet them for dinner?" she asked.

"Yes," Robin said, "I have to. I think it's best way to talk openly."

"What if you insult them?" Brenda asked. "What if they don't want to be friends anymore, after this?"

"I have you," Robin said. "You're the only friend I need, Bren. I'll be able to concentrate on you, and on my job."

"That's sweet, pal," Brenda said, "I love you, too, but what about good ol' Frank?"

"I think after I've done this I'll be able to sit down with Frank and talk to him, too."

"And tell him what?"

"How I feel."

"Rob?" Brenda said. She was the only one who ever

dropped the "in" from her name. "Do you know how you feel? I mean, you've only been separated a short time."

"I thought about it all last night, Bren," she said. "I—I think I need to live alone. I need my freedom again."

"Does this have anything to do with Mr. Perfect and his wife?" Brenda asked.

"No," Robin said, "well, yes, maybe. Maybe I just feel I need to see other people."

"Not them, necessarily?"

"No," Robin said, "just other . . . other men."

"How's Frank going to take this, Robin?"

"Hard," she said, "I know that."

"Poor Frank."

Robin knew that Brenda liked Frank. She'd read some of his books before Robin had introduced them, and all of them since. The two of them got along great, and she wondered idly, with Frank free, if Brenda would be interested? And if so, how would she feel about that?

And if she had to wonder that should she be married to Frank, at all?

"What time's dinner tonight?" Brenda asked.

"Seven."

"Where?"

"Duff's."

"Want to meet for a drink at Dressel's first?"

"No, Bren," Robin said, "I want to be stone sober for this. I think I'll just stick around here until about six-thirty and catch up on some work and then head over there."

"Well, all right," Brenda said, "but you've got to call me tonight and tell me what happened."

"I will."

"Promise?"

"I swear," Robin said.

"I'll be sitting by the phone."

"I said I'd call."

"Okay," Brenda said. "Good luck, then."

"Thanks."

"Oh, and Rob?"

"Yes?"

"Just in case you want to do it again don't feel—"

"Good-bye, Brenda."

She hung up, then shook her head and laughed at her friend's playful tone of voice. Brenda probably would have killed for a chance at a man like Vince Wheaton. Maybe that was Robin's solution. Maybe she should introduce Vince and Amy to Brenda? Her friend was tall, blonde, and beautiful, maybe they'd prefer her.

No, as tempting as that was—she would have loved to see Brenda's face when she met the couple—that wasn't the solution to her problem. She had to decide what she wanted to do, and then let the Wheatons know in no uncertain terms that what had happened four nights ago was not going to happen again. If they were insulted there was nothing she could do about it.

Just for a brief moment she thought about that night, about how Vince had looked naked—she'd caught her breath at the sight of him—how his mouth and hands had felt on her, how it had felt when she felt his penis sliding into her, that first, unexpected, surprising orgasm—but then, there in her memory, was Amy, watching her husband make love to Robin, and then there were Amy's hands, touching her—

She shook her head to dispel the image. The truth was every time she thought about it she became excited thinking about Vince, and then uncomfortable and embarrassed thinking about Amy. There was no way to get around it.

She had to tell them how she really felt.

EIGHT

Robin was oddly relieved to see that she had arrived first. This gave her the option of leaving before they arrived, if she decided to do so. She got them a table for three in Duff's main dining room. She loved eating there, felt at home with the hardwood floors and brick walls, and enjoyed the ever-changing, eclectic menu. She was even on their mailing list so she'd know when the menu changed from season to season.

When she met the Wheatons they had told her that they'd only been living in St. Louis a few months. The first time she went to lunch with them she'd taken them to Duff's, and they also fell in love with the place. It had been here where she'd introduced them to Frank, here where she'd had dinner with them and told them about her separation from Frank, and here where they'd had dinner the other night before . . .

Suddenly, there they were, approaching her table, each of them smiling, both just achingly beautiful people. She supposed she should have counted herself lucky that they'd even wanted her in that way . . .

She stood up and Vince was the first to greet her.

"Robin, sweetie," he said, kissing her cheek and then hugging her. She'd always liked the way his cologne smelled, but now it was as if it were the very essence of sex. She grew wet and tingly from his embrace, and this annoyed her.

Then he stepped aside and Amy was there. She took

Robin into her arms and hugged her, pressing their cheeks together. Robin stiffened in Amy's arms and wondered if the other woman noticed. Amy's perfume had always intrigued Robin, but now it panicked her. Her heart began to beat faster as she pulled away from the embrace, hoping that she wasn't being too obvious.

They all sat and a T-shirted waiter appeared at their table.

"Drink?" Vince asked Robin.

She was ready for that question. "Iced tea." She was going to stay very sober during this dinner. Besides, she loved the taste of Duff's spiced tea.

Vince ordered a pint of a local brew they had on draft and Amy asked for a white wine.

"Well," Vince said, when the waiter had left them, "how are you?"

"To tell you the truth," she said, "I'm a little nervous."

Vince and Amy exchanged a glance and Robin had the feeling that they'd made some prior arrangements for this meeting, and Vince was taking the lead.

"Please don't be," Vince said. "What happened with the three of us—well, we think it was just marvelous."

"Vince—"

"We understand if you feel awkward, though," Vince said.

"Awkward is one way of putting it," Robin said. "You see, I never expected . . . I mean, I didn't think . . ."

"You must have some idea how we feel about you, Robin," Vince said. "You must have had some clue."

"I thought we were *friends,* Vince, that's all," she said, "honestly."

"We are friends," Vince said, "we're great friends, but . . . I mean, to have come with us—"

Robin was grateful for the appearance of the waiter at that moment with their drinks. It kept Vince from saying what he was going to say and gave her a chance to think.

The waiter set down their drinks and asked if they were ready to order.

"We haven't looked at the menu, yet," Vince said.

"I can tell you about the specials—"

"We'll call you when we're ready!" Vince snapped and the waiter retreated. Robin had never seen Vince display even a hint of anger before, and it surprised her. Amy put her hand on her husband's arm, and he immediately calmed down. Though he was doing the talking, she seemed in charge.

"Vince—"

"No, really, Robin," Vince said, cutting her off, "we understand—"

"I don't think you do," Robin said. "I mean . . . I'm married, Vince. I may be separated, but I'm still married, and—"

"You don't love him," Amy said.

"What?" She stared at Amy, who was looking at her with an amused expression. "How do you know how I feel about my husband? What gives you the right—"

"Robin," Vince said, holding up one hand in a placating gesture, "please—"

"No," she said, "she doesn't have the right—"

"I'm sorry," Amy said, immediately, "you're right, I shouldn't have said it. That was insensitive of me. Please, I apologize."

"There," Vince said, "Amy's apologized." Robin watched as Vince gave Amy a warning glance. She'd never witnessed them exchange anything but loving looks, before. She realized she really didn't know these two people at all.

Even after months of dinner conversations, how could you know somebody well enough to . . . ?

"This can't happen again," Robin blurted.

"What?" Vince asked.

"What happened the other night can never happen again," she said. "I'm sorry, but I'm just not . . . not into that. I'm not that way."

"Robin," Vince said, "we have a solution."

"We can stay friends, if you like," Robin went on, thinking this was what they wanted to hear. Tell them what they wanted to hear and then make an excuse and *leave,* she was telling herself.

"Robin," Vince said, "of course we want to be friends, but we think we have a solution to this dilemma."

"A solution?" Robin said. "What solution?"

Vince looked at Amy, who nodded to him.

"We'd like you to come and live with us."

Robin stared at him.

"What?"

"We want you to move in with us," Vince said, "come live with us. Robin . . . we love you."

NINE

She couldn't believe what she was hearing.

"This is some sort of a joke, right?" she asked.

"It's no joke," Amy said.

"We're serious," Vince said.

Robin stared at them in turn for a few seconds and saw that they were, indeed, serious.

"You want me to come and . . . and live with you?"

"Very much," Vince said.

"As what?" she asked. "As . . . as some sort of pet, or something?"

"Not at all," Vince said. He seemed offended by the remark. "We want you to come as you are, a personable, dedicated, intelligent, very sensual woman."

Robin was speechless for a moment, she could only stammer, "I—I'm married."

"Well," Vince said, "you could get a divorce, if you want to, but it's not necessary as far as we're concerned."

Robin recalled a news story about some comedienne and her husband wanting them to marry another woman and bring her into their home. Robin had thought it an incredible story, but this . . . this was amazing.

"If you people are serious about this . . ." Robin said.

"We are," Vince replied.

". . . then I think there is something very wrong—"

Amy stood up abruptly and looked down at Robin who, for the moment, was stunned into silence. Was Amy going to hit her? Shout at her?

"I'm going to the ladies room," Amy said, and turned and walked away.

As soon as Amy was absent Vince reached out and took Robin's right hand in both of his.

"Robin, darling," he said, "what happened the other night can be the beginning. We truly want this. We'll treat you very well, I promise."

"Vince," she said, looking into his beautiful blue eyes, "if it was just you asking . . . I mean, if you were asking me to be with you . . . move in with you without Amy . . . but even that would be—"

Suddenly, Vince released her hand and sat back. The move was so abrupt that Robin stopped and stared at him. She didn't like what she saw. His eyes looked puzzled and he looked . . . well, *appalled* was the only word she could think of.

"Ask you to move in with me?" he said. "Without Amy?"

"It was just a . . . a . . ."

"Why would I do that?" Vince asked, incredulously. "I love Amy and she loves me. That would be . . . cheating on her."

Robin stared at him, helpless. Speechless. He truly seemed so offended.

"I would *never* cheat on Amy, Robin."

"But . . . but you were with me the other night—"

"*We* were with you," he corrected her. "And we want you to move in with us. I could never leave Amy to be with you, or anyone."

"But then . . . why would you want . . . want this . . . if you're so happy together?"

"We're very happy together," he said, "but that doesn't mean we can't share that happiness with another person," he said. "We'd never leave each other, but we would bring someone else in to live with us. We want you to be that person."

Robin shook her head and said, "I don't understand . . . I can't understand this . . . if only it was a joke."

"It's not a joke," Vince said, staring at her, his eyes suddenly going cold. "We are serious about this, Robin," he said, "deadly serious."

Looking into his eyes she was suddenly convinced that he was mad—and if he was crazy, so was Amy.

"I—I have to go," she said, grabbing her purse.

"Robin!" He grabbed her wrist.

"Let go, Vince."

"You haven't given us your answer."

"My answer?" she asked, and now it was she who was incredulous. "My answer is no! What else could it be? This . . . this proposal of yours is . . . is madness."

Vince stared at her, his eyes narrowed, his grip on her wrist tightening.

"Vince," she said, "you're hurting me."

He didn't let go. Robin hated scenes, but she was afraid she might have to create one to get away.

"Robin," he said, slowly, "we are going to give you time to think this over, to get over the . . . the surprise of it."

She decided she had to play along with him just to get him to let her go.

"All right, Vince," she said, "all right, I'll think it over. Now . . . let go of my wrist. I have to leave."

They stared at each other for a few moments and then, just as abruptly as his attitude had changed, it did so again. He released her, smiled and he was charming Vince again.

"Jesus," she said, "you *are* crazy."

"Rob—"

She moved away from the table before he could grab her

again. In her haste to get out she almost ran right into Amy, who was returning from the ladies room.

"Robin, wha—"

"You're crazy," Robin said to her, "you're both crazy."

She ran out, then, unmindful and uncaring of whether or not she had created a scene. All she wanted to do was get away.

Amy returned to the table and sat down next to her husband, who took her hand.

"That didn't go well," she said.

"Not as we planned, at all."

"She was shocked," she said, "that's all. We'll have to give her some time. Don't worry, dear." She put her arm around him. "She'll come around . . . she has to . . ."

" . . . or else," Vince said.

She smiled.

"Exactly."

Robin tightened her grip on her mug of tea but it did little to stop the shaking. Brenda sat across from her. They were in Brenda's kitchen. She needed to talk to someone, and she certainly could not talk to Frank about this. Brenda was the only one who knew all of the facts.

"Do you want anything else?" Brenda asked.

"No," Robin, said, "this is good."

"Something stronger?"

Robin shook her head and gave her friend a wan smile. "No, this is fine. I . . . just needed somebody to talk to."

"Well, then," Brenda said, "talk to me, girl."

Robin took a deep breath and hesitated. She still wasn't sure if it had all happened the way she thought it did. Had she somehow misunderstood what had happened, what had been said?

"Robin?"

"I'm sorry, Bren," she said, startled. "I still can't believe it happened."

"Well," Brenda said, "you're going to have to tell me *what* happened before I can have an opinion."

Robin took a deep breath and said, "okay," and told Brenda what happened . . .

When Robin finished her story Brenda sat back in her chair and said, "Wow."

"I know."

"I can't believe it."

"I *know.*"

"That's quite an offer."

"From two crazy people!" Robin said.

"Well, yeah . . . but gorgeous people."

"Bren!"

"I'm just saying, Robin," Brenda replied, "some people would kill for an offer like that."

"Not me."

"Well, you've been pretty surprising of late," Brenda said. "You've got to admit that."

"Well, I'm cured. My adventurous days are over."

"Are you afraid of them?" Brenda asked. "Do you think they're . . . a danger to you?"

"I don't think so," Robin said. "I don't know . . . they're obviously very different people from who I thought they were. But . . . I don't know if they're dangerous."

Brenda reached across the table to take her friend's hands and found them ice cold. "Boy, this really has you spooked, huh?"

"You didn't see them, Brenda," Robin said. "You didn't

see his eyes when he thought I was telling him to leave his wife."

"It's nice to find a man who's that faithful, though," Brenda said, "I mean, in this day and age."

"Brenda."

"I don't know how to react to this, Robin," Brenda said, in her own defense. "I suppose you did the right thing and now they're out of your life—if that was what you wanted."

"It is!" Robin insisted. "If you want some excitement in your life I'll be glad to introduce you to them."

"Oh, sure," Brenda said, "now you want to introduce me."

The two friends stared at each other across the table and then suddenly the tension broke and they started to laugh.

"See?" Brenda said, when she could. "This is why you called me."

"Oh, Bren," Robin said, "I don't know what I'd do without you."

"Hopefully," Brenda said, "you'll never have to find out."

TEN

It was a week before Robin saw the Wheatons again.

It had been a good week. She'd been concentrating on her job, had a good dinner with Frank where they talked a bit about what they were doing but not where they were going—that conversation would come later—and she had not heard from either Vince or Amy Wheaton, at all.

For a few days after their dinner she would jump whenever the phone rang at home or at work, but by the fourth day when she didn't hear Vince's voice on the other end of the phone she thought, it's over.

But a week to the day that the Wheatons made their offer Robin got out of her car and walked to the steps of the museum. Her arms were full of files she had brought home to go over and her purse was over her shoulder. She started to ascend when she suddenly saw them. They were just standing there out in the open, right at the base of the statue of St. Louis, apparently watching her.

As she hurried to go up the steps she missed one and the heel on her shoe snapped off. She stumbled, dropped the files and almost fell, righted herself and looked at the Wheatons again. They hadn't moved, were not coming forward and now she felt like a fool as she leaned over to pick up the heel of her shoe and the scattered files. They were just watching, with no apparent intent to approach her.

Robin went up the steps with as much dignity as she could muster and entered the building. Once inside she stopped and leaned against a wall with her eyes closed and tried to regulate her breathing.

"Are you all right, Robin?"

She opened her eyes and looked at one of the guards. His name was Raymond; a man in his sixties who'd always showed fatherly concern toward Robin since she first started working there.

She blew her bangs off her forehead. "I'm okay, Ray. Broke a heel off my shoe." She held it up to show him. "Could've broken my neck, I guess."

"You have to be more careful," Ray told her. "We don't want to lose you."

"Thank you, Ray," she said. "I don't want to lose me, either."

She gathered herself, adjusted the files in her arms, clutched her broken heel in one hand and then limped off down the hall towards her office.

Her office window overlooked the front of the museum. From time to time she looked out the window and saw Vince and Amy, still standing there, still watching the building. As far as she could tell they hadn't moved since she got there.

After the fifth or sixth look out the window it was three in the afternoon. She'd had lunch in the museum cafeteria so as not to go outside and let them see her again. Now she wondered if she should call security. Did they have the authority to make them leave? Or should she call the police? And tell them what? That a couple she'd ill advisedly had sex with once were standing in front of the museum?

She decided to wait until it was time for her to leave to make a decision. At four forty-five she looked out the window again and was pleased and surprised to see that the couple was gone.

She had changed into a pair of shoes she kept in a bottom desk drawer in case of an emergency. She decided to wear those home and put the pair with the broken heel into a plastic bag to take home.

She walked to the front door of the museum, said goodnight to Ray and went outside. She stopped on the top step to take a look around, but Vince and Amy were nowhere in sight. She went down the steps and walked to her car. There was something on her windshield, pinned beneath the wiper, probably a flier for a new take-out restaurant or home carpet cleaning business. When she got closer she saw that it was a powder blue envelope with her name written on the front. From the looks of it, it was a greeting card of some kind. She would have thought it was from Frank, but the handwriting did not look like his.

She took the card off the window and got into the car. She put her purse on the passenger seat, put her key in the ignition and then opened the envelope.

The picture on the card was one of those with a little boy and a little girl holding hands and kissing. In this photo both were wearing adult hats and looking precious. On the card it said: "Thinking of you." When she opened the card she saw the word, "ALWAYS," in capital letters. Beneath it was written, "Love, Vince & Amy."

Abruptly she hit the button on her car door that controlled the locks. She looked around first to make sure no one was in the car, and then to see if anyone was around it. She was alone, but that didn't make her relax. They'd been in front of the museum all day, and then before they left they put this card on her windshield. What were they telling her, that they weren't going away? And once again, how could she go to the police? What would she tell them, that someone had left her a greeting card?

She dropped the card on the seat next to her purse and started the car. She backed out of her spot and started for home. Maybe they'd go away, after a while, once she didn't change her mind or respond to them in any way.

If they didn't, then she didn't know what she was going to do.

"I don't know what to tell you, Robin," Brenda said.

Robin moved her Pasta-in-a-Bowl around and then pushed it away from her.

"I can't go to the police, Bren," she said into the phone.

"You keep saying that," Brenda said. "Why don't you just go and talk to somebody? Maybe they can do something?"

"What do I tell them?" she asked. "I had sex with a man and a woman I hardly knew?"

"It sounds terrible when you put it that way," Brenda said. "Just tell them you're being stalked."

"And who do I tell them is stalking me?" Robin asked.

"Give them the names, Vince and Amy . . . what is it? . . . Wheaton."

"And who do I tell them they are?"

"Acquaintances," Brenda said. "Lie to them, Robin. They're cops; they've been lied to before. Tell them you met them at a party and they won't leave you alone."

"I don't know, Bren," Robin said. "I don't know . . . maybe they won't be there tomorrow."

"Fine," Brenda said, "then wait a while and see what happens. If you still see them, if they make contact in any way—in person, on the phone, another damn card—then go to the police."

"I feel better talking to you," Robin said. "Thanks."

"Robin? What about Frank?"

"W-what about him?"

"Have you thought about talking to him?"

"We talked a couple of nights ago," Robin said. "We had dinner. We had a good talk, too. How good do you think it would have been if I told him about all this?"

"Robin, why don't you just tell him they're bothering you?" Brenda suggested. "Don't tell him what happened."

"Lie to him, lie to the cops," Robin said. "I've never been a good liar, Bren."

Brenda let out a sigh and said, "I know, kiddo. That's my department."

"I didn't mean—"

"No, I'm serious. I lie to men all the time. I'm good at it. I could teach you. Or if you want me to do it for you—"

Robin cut her off by laughing and then said, "You're good for me, Bren."

"Anything you need," Brenda said, "all you have to do is call, you hear?"

"I hear."

"Get some sleep."

"I will," Robin said. "Thanks."

After they hung up Robin dumped the rest of the microwave pasta in the trash. She tried watching some T.V. but couldn't concentrate. Then she tried to read a book, but that didn't work out any better.

She went into her bedroom and turned on the light in her walk-in closet. She'd always wanted a walk-in closet and when she found this apartment complex off of Gravois Road in South County she grabbed it, even though she wasn't sure she was going to be able to afford it.

Stepping into the closet she immediately felt insulated against the outside world. This was something she got from this closet that she didn't expect. She began to look at her clothes, just running her hands over them. She'd bought very few new things in the two months she'd been living here, and the closet was only half full. If she went back to Frank she'd have to give it up. If she didn't go back she wondered how long it would take her, on her salary, to get it full.

Unfortunately, she couldn't stay in the closet forever. She picked out her nightclothes and closed the twin doors. She found herself watching the phone, waiting for it to ring. If it did she knew her heart would leap into her throat. Finally, she decided to unplug the phone and go to bed.

ELEVEN

As she left her apartment the next morning an envelope that had been stuck in the door fell to the floor. She knew that the apartment complex board left a copy of their minutes in the door of every tenant, but this wasn't that kind of envelope.

This was a greeting card envelope.

This one was pink, and she stared at it for a few seconds, inches from the toes of her shoes, before she bent over and picked it up. For a moment she was paralyzed by indecision. Should she unlock her door, go back inside and read it, or read it out here in the hall. No, she would run back inside. She looked up and down the hall. There were three other apartments on her floor, but no one was in the hall. She opened the envelope and took out the card. The front was a black and white photo of a man and a woman, both wearing white T-shirts and jeans. They were in a hot embrace, kissing. There were no words on the front, though. When she opened it she saw the words, "Don't worry, we'll make out." It was signed, "Love, Vince & Amy." It was innocuous enough to be frightening.

She closed the card, returned it to the envelope and then put the envelope into her purse. They were playing with her, trying to frighten her, but she wasn't going to give them that satisfaction.

Time to go to work.

When she got outside and started walking towards her car she saw them. They were in their car in a parking space across from her building, and they were watching her from the front seat. She tried not to run the rest of the way to her car, but her steps did quicken. She flushed when she dropped her keys as she was trying to fit the key into the door lock. She hated being flustered, and that they were witnessing it. She got the door open, got into her car, started the motor and drove away watching her rear view mirror.

They did not seem to be following her.

She pulled into her parking space and walked to the museum steps. They were standing in the same place they were the day before. She had no idea how they had gotten here before her. She found herself wishing old St. Louis would reach down from his horse and smite them. Then just for a second she thought about waving to them, to show that she wasn't intimidated, but she turned and went up the stairs and into the museum.

" 'Mornin', Robin," Ray said, smiling.

"Good morning, Ray."

"All your heels intact, this morning?" the older man asked.

"What? Oh, yes, thanks. I was more careful this morning."

"Glad to hear it." He actually tipped his cap to her. She thought he must have been a very dashing man when he was younger. "Have a nice day."

"You, too, Ray."

She turned and went down the hall to her office. Once there she looked out her window. They were there, just standing. From here they looked like two little perfect dolls, like Barbie and Ken.

She went back to her desk and tried to concentrate on her work. Opening a drawer for the first time that day she froze when she saw the orange greeting card envelope. With trembling hands she took it out and opened it. The card had three people on the front, a man and two women, and they were naked. The novelty card had famous heads grafted onto naked, grotesquely endowed bodies. There was nothing written on the front, but when she opened it she saw a traffic sign that would normally say ONE-WAY, only this one said "Three-Way." The card was signed "Love, V&A."

She took the other greeting cards out of her bag and set them side-by-side on top of her desk. They had left one on her car, one in her door at home and, somehow, had gotten into her office to leave one in her desk. How long before they broke *into* her home to leave one—and then what was next?

If she waited to go to the police, say a week to ten days, and was then forced to go to them they might ask her why she waited so long? And she knew that if she went to them she'd have to tell them the whole story. She was a terrible liar, as she had told Brenda, plus she'd want to show them all three cards, and not just the first two.

She stacked the greeting cards and picked up the telephone. Why wait until their behavior escalated into something else. Even if the police couldn't do anything directly to the Wheatons, maybe somebody could give her some advice on how to handle this?

It had to stop before it went too far.

TWELVE

Detective Jack Jones put his hand on the doorknob and found the front door of the house unlocked. Front doors of homes should never be unlocked. For a cop, that was always a bad sign, especially when he was responding to a report of a crime.

He opened the door and entered the house, his hand on his gun. He closed the door behind him and made sure it was locked, then started up the stairs to the second floor. Normally, he would have called out to see if anyone was home, but he went up the stairs quietly, listening intently for any sound from the second floor.

When he reached the top step he could see the doorways to three different rooms. He moved down the hall, bypassed the first door and went to the second. When he looked inside he saw the woman. She was as rumpled as the bed, but a hell of a lot better looking. She had long red hair, very pale skin, and she was showing a lot of it. She was wearing a kimono type garment, but it was in a state of disarray so that he could see her shoulders and one full, smooth breast. Also, it only reached the very tops of her thighs, so her long, muscular legs were very much in evidence.

Her head was down as he entered and abruptly she brought it up, saw him and gasped. Her eyes were emerald green, amazing eyes that bored into him as he stood there in the doorway.

"Ma'am," he said.

"Who are you?" she demanded. "How did you get in?"

"Take it easy," he said, taking his wallet out. "I'm a police officer, see?" he showed her his badge. "As to how I got in, the front door was unlocked."

"Oh," she said. She brushed some hair from her face, a move that revealed more of her left breast, enough so that he could see that her nipples were a coppery color. He only saw one, but it was a pretty safe assumption that both were the same color. "He must have left it unlocked."

"Who's that, Ma'am?" he asked, putting his wallet away. He was aware of his erection, not fully extended yet, but getting there. The room smelled of her, her perfume, her shampoo, her sex.

"The man."

"What man?"

"The man who . . . assaulted me."

She didn't looked bruised, just mussed, so he asked what any cop would ask.

"Uh, Ma'am, by assault do you mean . . ."

"Raped."

"He raped you?"

"Yes," she said, "but he . . . made me . . . do things to him, first."

Any man who looked at this woman—tall, pale, red-haired, built, sexy as hell, in her early twenties—would know that she could "do" a lot of things to a man.

"What kind of things, Ma'am?"

"Just . . . things . . . dirty things."

He noticed she was staring at the bulge in his crotch, and he thought there was a hungry look in her eyes. The door was locked downstairs, and he had not called for backup. He moved away from the doorway and closer to her, trying to remember what came next.

"Could you describe these things to me?"

"Oh, no," she said, looking away, "no, I . . . I couldn't."

"Well then," he said, his hands going to his belt, "I think maybe you should show me . . ."

"You forgot some of your lines, Jack," Katherine Jones told her husband, after they had each caught their breath.

"Jesus," he said, lying next to her, on his back, "I'm gonna have a heart attack one of these days and you're worried about me forgetting some lines."

"Oh, come on, old timer," she said, "it's all I can do to keep up with *you*."

"You're a sweet, generous young thing, Katy." *Very* young, he thought. Twenty-two to his forty-three. He didn't know what he was thinking when he married her. Yes, he did, but he didn't know what *she* was thinking marrying *him*. Actually, she had *saved* his life by marrying him, but everyone on the job thought he was crazy to marry a stripper twenty years younger than he was. He could have told them different but he didn't feel that any of them was worth the time it would take to explain to them that she was the only good thing that had happened to him in all that time.

But with no cases to catch he had more time to sneak home during the day and play sex games with his incredible young wife.

"I don't think you should let your gun drop to the floor like that," she said, then. "What if it went off and shot one of us? How would we explain that?"

That wasn't going to happen, he knew, but to mollify her he said, "Next time I'll take it off and put it on the night table, or something."

"Okay," she said. "Well, I'm getting my second wind here, old man. What's next? I could get my dominatrix outfit out."

"Oh, man," he said, "save that one for your customers, Katy. You going to work tonight?" She worked at one of the strip joints out in Collinsville, just across the bridge from St. Louis.

"Yeah, I told Leo I'd put in a few hours."

"Well, then, you'll need some rest before then, won't you?"

She reached over and took him in her hand and said, "I don't think I'm the one who needs to rest, Jack."

He was about to answer her when the phone on the bedside table rang.

"Fuck!" she swore. "What timing."

"Play time is over, sweetie," he said. "Hand me the phone. It might be the office."

Detective Jack Jones' wife rolled over, grabbed the phone and passed it to him reluctantly.

THIRTEEN

When he entered the office he was surprised to find it empty. The team assigned to catching cases that day must have already been called out. Before checking in with the Captain he walked over to the IN box to see what cases had come in when Phillips came out of his office and spotted him.

"Just the man I'm looking for. I've got a job for you."

"Cap?" Jones couldn't believe his ears. The cop who'd called him at home to tell him the Captain wanted him didn't tell him why. There was a tone in the man's voice he hadn't heard in months.

"I just got a call from the Chief," Phillips said. "Some lady at the Museum of Art is complaining about stalkers, or something. Go and talk to her, keep her happy. The Mayor is a contributor."

"Me?"

"You see anyone else? Wasn't that you asking to be put back on the chart last week so you could start catching cases again?"

"Keep some princess at the Museum happy? That's a case?"

"Well, you could just stay here and continue to do paperwork."

"Never mind," Jones said, "I'll go . . ."

"Mrs. Lobianco?"

The woman looked up from her desk. She was pretty,

although her features did seem to be a bit mismatched.

"Yes?"

"Detective Jack Jones."

"Oh, Detective," she said, standing up. She'd made the call to the police only that morning, and here was a detective in her office at four in the afternoon. She obviously hadn't expected such quick service. Apparently she didn't know that the mention of the Museum had raised a red flag in the computer system. There were several red flags like that; all placed there at the Mayor's instructions when he first took office. He wanted his political cronies taken care of.

"You look surprised," he said.

"No—I mean, yes, I am," she said, standing and extending her hand, which he shook. "I guess I didn't expect them to send a detective to talk to me about stalkers."

"That makes two of us," he said.

"Excuse me?" Robin asked.

"I'm with the Major Case Squad, Mrs. Lobianco," he explained. "Normally, this wouldn't qualify as something I'd work on."

"I see," she said. "Then . . . uh, why are you here?"

"The Art Museum is an important part of the City, Ma'am," he said. "My bosses want to keep your bosses happy." He spread his arms in a gesture of supplication. "So here I am."

"I see," she said, in a different tone. "So you don't want to be here."

"No, Ma'am, I don't," he said, "but when I get called to the scene of a homicide I don't really want to be there, either. I do my job, though, no matter what."

"I can appreciate your honesty, Detective," she said. "Won't you sit down?"

"Thank you."

"Coffee, or tea or . . . something else?"

He shook his head and said, "That won't be necessary. Why don't we get to it?"

"All right," she said, seating herself behind her desk.

"Why don't you tell me about these stalkers."

"How much do you know?"

He smiled, unaware that she thought it took a few years off his age and some of the hardness out of his face.

"Why don't you just explain it to me as if I didn't know anything about it, at all?" he asked.

He took out a small spiral notebook, a pen, and waited.

Jones listened intently to the story the woman told him. She appeared sheepish when she told how she had willingly accepted Vince and Amy Wheaton as friends, embarrassed when she told of the night of sex she had shared with them, and then angry when speaking of the greeting cards they had left for her. He felt she was being totally honest and leaving nothing out, although it was not easy for her.

When she was finished the detective stood up and walked to the window. He didn't see anyone standing out in front of the museum at the moment, just some people entering and leaving.

"Do you still have the cards?" he asked, turning back to face her.

"Yes," she said, opening a drawer, "I kept them. I touched them, but nobody else has . . . in case you want to get fingerprints."

He smiled as he approached the desk.

"There won't be any need for fingerprinting if they signed them, Mrs. Lobianco."

Now she looked sheepish again. "Yes, of course. How silly of me."

He stared down at the cards, as she had spread them on the desk. His eyes fell on the nude bodies on the cover of the last one. He recalled that afternoon, as he was getting dressed to go back to work, that his wife had been standing in front of the mirror, examining her own nude body . . .

"I think I need new implants, Jack," she'd said, turning and shaking her boobs at him. "I jiggled too much today."

"You jiggle just fine, babe. You're still the most requested lap dance at the club, aren't you?"

"Yeah, but there are younger girls coming in all the time," she said. "You know, I'm no spring chicken anymore."

"All of twenty-two," he said.

"Twenty-three next month."

"Hell," he'd said, "I better start looking for a replacement."

"What do you think?" Robin asked, jerking him back from his reverie.

He took the time to open each card and read the inside before answering.

"Mrs. Lobianco," he said, "at this point there's not much I can do. I can't arrest people for sending you greeting cards."

"I know that," she said. "I knew that when I called you."

"What did you expect to have done then?"

"I just . . . wanted some advice," she said, with a shrug. "I don't know how to handle this."

"Have you discussed it with your husband?"

"Detective Jones," she said, "you heard my story, and I've told you the whole truth. You were nice enough not to react when I told you about . . . about being with them."

That was because he was married to a stripper, a woman

who made her living in the sex industry. Threesomes did not shock him.

"So you realize that I could hardly tell my husband about any of this. Besides, we're separated."

"Perhaps, if you had a man around, it would dissuade these two from pursuing you."

"Are you suggesting I hire a bodyguard?" she asked. "I don't have the money for that."

"I wasn't suggesting that at all," he said.

"Well, please," she said, "suggest something."

He sighed and looked down at the cards again. Keep her happy, his boss, Captain Phillips, had said. He sat back down.

"Have they followed you?"

"No."

"Have they called you on the phone?"

"Not since the cards have come," she said. "Not in the past few days, no."

"There are new laws being drafted all the time. What about e-mail? Have they sent you any sexually explicit or threatening e-mail?"

"E-mail," she said. "I haven't checked my e-mail in two days."

He looked at the computer on her desk.

"Do you get it here and at home?"

"Yes."

"Can you check both from here?"

"Yes, I can."

"Why don't we do that now?" he asked. "It might give us more ammunition to work with."

"All right," she said, turning her computer on. "It'll take a few minutes."

"That's fine."

While she logged into her computer and got on line he

leaned forward to look at the cards again. The one with the nude bodies was a novelty card. The bodies were not actually doing anything explicit, but he wondered if the card could qualify as something sexually explicit that had been sent—but no, it hadn't been sent through the mail. He sat back. That angle was out.

He heard the computer tell her, "Hello," first and then "You've got mail."

"I'll check my office account first," she said. The keyboard keys clicked quickly beneath her fingers and while she concentrated on the monitor he concentrated on her. He could see why a man would be attracted to her. While she was not as beautiful as she said this couple was, and not as overtly sexy as his own wife, she certainly had an attractive quality to her face, and a body that would interest any man—and some women, obviously.

"Okay," she said, "there's nothing from them on my office account. Let me bring up my home account."

He waited as she clicked, and then she sighed and sat back.

"Nothing?" he asked.

"No."

"All right," he said, "keep checking it every day."

"I usually do," she said, "I've just been . . . so distracted lately."

"Mrs. Lobianco," he said, "I'd suggest that you keep a log."

"A log? Of what?"

"Of the times you see them outside here or your home," he said. "Also, log in and save every card you get. Write down how you got it, where and when. Specifically, let me know if you get something in the mail or through e-mail."

"What will this accomplish?"

"It will establish a pattern," he said, "which, in the future, may be of use if and when these people are arrested."

"You can arrest them?"

"Not without probable cause, Ma'am."

"And what would that be?"

"Well, I'm not completely up on stalking laws because they're so new, and they vary from state to state, but I believe that it would largely be up to you."

"Me?" she said, putting her hand to her throat in an age old, feminine gesture. "You would arrest them on my say so?"

"I'll do some research on the law so that I don't advise you wrong, Ma'am, but—"

"Could you stop calling me 'Ma'am'?" she asked, abruptly. "I just—it makes me nervous, for some reason. Like you were Jack Webb, or somebody."

"All right."

"Call me Robin, or Mrs. Lobianco, whichever you like, but not . . . Ma'am?"

"You got it, Robin," Jones said, opting for the more familiar. "As I was saying, I'll research it so I don't advise you wrongly but I believe that you have to be in fear for your safety."

"Oh."

"I know you said you've been distracted because of this, but are you in fear?"

She thought a moment and then replied honestly.

"No," she said, "not in fear for my life . . ."

"And if we arrested you'd have to testify against them."

"I see."

"There's another thing," he said, "and I'm only telling you this because you seem concerned about your husband finding out about all of this."

"What is it?"

"Well, it's my understanding that stalking is broken up into three categories. There's Stranger Stalking, Acquaintance Stalking, and Intimate Stalking."

It took her a few seconds to assimilate what he was saying. When she did she said, "Oh."

"You understand."

She nodded.

"According to what I've told you," she replied, "this would be an intimate stalking."

"Yes," he said, "or, to be more precise, a former intimate stalking, meaning that you are being stalked by a person or persons you have formerly been intimate with."

"And that would come out in court?"

"Yes."

"I see," she said. "I'll have to think about that."

"And the final thing is . . . I'm not all that sure we have a stalking case, here. I mean, it's only been a few days."

"I see."

"Start that log," he said, getting to his feet, "and let me know about the mail and e-mail situation."

"All right," she said. "Let me walk you out of the building."

"Thank you."

They walked together to the front entrance of the museum.

"Have you been here before?" she asked.

"No," he said, "but I keep meaning to come."

"Never came as a child?"

"I didn't grow up here in St. Louis," he said. "I've only lived here half my life."

"I grew up here," she said. "I love this place, and I always wanted to work here. Now I do and I'm not doing my job the way I should be."

"Because of this situation?"

She nodded.

When they reached the front door Ray looked concerned and asked Robin, "Is everything all right?"

"Fine, Ray," she said, "nothing to worry about."

They stepped outside into the sunlight and stopped.

"You should probably let security know what's going on," Jones said.

"I can't do that," she said, "even though they were somehow able to get into my office and leave a card in my desk."

"Not necessarily," he said. "They could have paid someone to do it. Do you have an assistant?"

"No," she said.

"But there are other employees who could have done it."

"Yes . . . but still, I can't . . . I don't want my boss . . ."

"Robin, can I be blunt?"

"Of course."

"You're going to have to make a decision sooner or later," he said. "If this escalates into something we can arrest them for you'll have to decide to either protect your reputation—and your marriage—or prosecute them."

"I know."

"Think about it," he said. He took out a business card, then two, as an afterthought.

"Call me if you need anything."

"I only need one," she said.

"Take the other one," he said, "and write down the address of Vince and Amy Wheaton."

"What are you going to do?" she asked. He gave her a pen and she wrote the address down. "You said you couldn't—I mean, I don't want you to arrest them—"

He smiled and said, "Don't worry. I'll just go and meet

them and have a little talk. Maybe I can convince them to leave you alone and you won't have to deal with the possibility of prosecution."

"You . . . you don't have to do that."

"I won't if you tell me not to," he said. "I just want to see if I can do a little more for you than I'm required to."

"That's very . . . uh, okay, yes, I think I would like you to do that. If we can put a stop to this now . . . thank you, Detective Jones."

He smiled again and they shook hands.

"I'll be in touch," he said, and went down the stairs. Robin watched him until he was out of sight, then turned and went back into the museum.

FOURTEEN

Jack Jones wondered what it had been about Robin Lobianco that had made him decide to go and question Vince Wheaton and his wife, Amy. Perhaps it was simply the fact that he thought she was a nice lady, and nice people shouldn't have to put up with stalkers.

On the other hand, would a nice lady have had sex with the Wheatons in the first place? That question was probably best asked of and answered by a police detective who was married to a stripper half his age. It didn't matter what Robin—or any woman—had done prior to calling the "relationship" quits. Once a woman said no, that should have been the end of it. Jones knew that dozens of men a night looked at his wife as she danced naked, or sat in their laps, and didn't think of her as a "nice girl." Katy was, indeed, a nice girl, albeit one who stripped for a living and had some questionable garments and toys in her closet at home.

On the other hand, maybe he was just doing it because his boss had told him to keep the lady happy.

The address Robin Lobianco had given him was a house in the affluent Ladue section of St. Louis. Some of the homes along Ladue Rd. were mansions, but the one the Wheatons were living in was somewhat smaller than most. It was as if they had wanted to live in the area, but could not afford one of the larger homes. This gave them a manageable monthly bill and enabled them to say they lived in Ladue.

On the way to meet them Jones had used his radio to run a check on the Wheatons. He did not yet have the results back. Hopefully, it would be waiting for him when he got back to his office.

He drove down their driveway and parked in front of the large brick home that was entirely too modern looking for that area. Many of the homes had a charming look to them, a personality that this austere building lacked. There was a garage off to his right, which no doubt housed whatever car the Wheatons chose to drive. The door was closed, at the moment.

He walked to the front door and rang the bell. He got out his badge and I.D. so he'd be prepared to show it. The door was opened by absolutely the most exquisite woman he'd ever seen. She was small, lucky if she was over five feet, but perfectly shaped. It was easy to see this as she was wearing tight jeans and a skin tight T-shirt with some sort of design on the front. He couldn't make it out and decided it must be abstract. He also decided he'd better stop looking at the woman's small, perky breasts. If she worked at the club with Katy she'd give his wife a run for her money as the most popular lap dance, but Katy's breasts were larger—much larger—and that would probably give her the edge in a strip club. It took another moment for him to realize she looked a lot like—

"I get that a lot," she said, gazing up at him with violet eyes.

"Get what?"

"Shania Twain," the woman said, as if she'd read his mind. "That's what you were thinking, wasn't it?"

"Uh, well, yeah . . . except for the hair."

"Darker, I know," the woman said. "Can I help you?"

"Detective Jones, Ma'am," he said, displaying his badge and I.D.

"Is something wrong, Detective?" she asked, putting a perfectly manicured hand to her chest. "Are we making too much noise?"

"I don't know," Jones said, "what have you been doing?"

"Well, I'm not going to tell you," she said, coolly, "after all, you are the police."

"Are you Mrs. Wheaton? Amy Wheaton?"

"That's right."

"Is your husband home, Mrs. Wheaton?"

"Uh-uh," she said, "I should have known. Vince has been naughty, hasn't he?"

"I'd really like to speak to you both, if I can come in?"

"Well, of course," she said, "what sort of hostess would I be if I didn't invite the police in?"

She backed away to allow him to enter, but not far enough that he didn't have to run up against her to get by. She had an amused expression on her face as her breasts brushed him, and then she closed the door and turned to face him.

"We're in the den, Detective. Will you follow me?"

She led the way and from the way she moved her hips and butt she knew he was watching. What man wouldn't?

"Darling," she said, as they entered the den, "this is Detective Jones, if you can believe that."

"Really?" the man asked. "Jones? Is that for real?"

"He showed me his identification."

The man turned to face Jones and extended his hand. Jones found himself looking at a man he knew most women would fall into bed with at a moment's notice. He was tall, extremely handsome, and athletically built without being muscle-bound. In short, he was the perfect match for his wife. Why wouldn't Robin Lobianco fall into bed with them?

"Mr. Wheaton?" Jones asked, as they shook hands.

"Vince, please," Vince Wheaton said. "Can we get you a drink, Detective? Coffee, perhaps?"

"I'll have to get it myself," Amy told him. "The maid's day off."

"That's okay," Jones said. "I'll pass, thanks. I just need to take up a little bit of your time."

"Very well," Vince said. "I hope you won't mind if we have a drink?"

"No, go ahead."

There was a small but fully stocked bar against one wall. Vince went and got behind it while Amy perched on a barstool in front of it. She crossed her legs and Jones noticed for the first time that her tiny feet were bare. His eyes hadn't gone that far down before.

Vince poured what appeared to be white wine for both him and his wife. He was also wearing jeans, like his wife, but instead of a T-shirt he wore a casual sports shirt, short sleeved and open-necked. Neither of them wore any jewelry. Jones' detective's mind noticed these things and just filed them away.

"What can we do for you, Detective?" Vince asked.

"I believe the two of you are acquainted with Robin Lobianco?"

The two exchanged a glance, then Amy laughed and said, "Of course we are. Robin's one of our dearest friends."

Jones couldn't help but wonder if they went to bed with many of their "dearest friends."

"Well, it seems she's been receiving some disturbing, uh, cards at her home and at work from the two of you. Can you explain that to me?"

They exchanged another glance, as if they communicated with each other telepathically before one of them answered a question. This time it was Vince.

"Disturbing?" Vince asked. "We sent some cards, but I don't see where they'd be disturbing to anyone . . . do you, dear?"

"Vince, I told you that last one was over the top," Amy said, scolding her husband. "It had some nudity in it, but I never thought Robin was a prude."

They had first hand proof that she wasn't, but Jones didn't comment on that.

"Well, we had no idea our cards would upset her," Vince said.

"They were harmless enough," Amy said. "Why would she complain about them?"

"Well, according to Mrs. Lobianco," Jones said, "she called your friendship off. In fact, she rejected a rather odd offer from you."

"An offer?" Vince asked, after exchanging a glance with his wife. Jones was trying to read these looks, but couldn't. "What offer does she say we made?"

"I think you both know what I'm talking about," Jones said.

"I'm afraid we don't, Detective," Vince said, "and if you don't mind me saying so, this doesn't seem to be the kind of thing someone of your stature would be assigned to look into." Jones instinctively knew that Wheaton was trying to snow him.

"No? Oh, I see what you mean," Jones said. "No, it's my boss. See, the Art Museum is very important to the city of St. Louis. My superiors just want to keep everyone happy." Not wanting the couple to think there was anything personal going on—which, surprisingly, there was. He didn't like them, at all.

"I'm at a loss to explain this," Amy said.

"That's all right, Mrs. Wheaton," Jones said, "I didn't expect you to actually admit to stalking her."

"Stalking—" Vince blurted, but Amy waved a hand and he fell silent. Jones thought that he'd just gotten some insight into who the dominant partner in this relationship was.

"No one is stalking anyone, Detective," Amy said. "Frankly, I'm shocked by this turn of events, but if Robin wanted to end our friendship all she had to do was say so."

"She says she did," Jones replied, "in no uncertain terms."

"Well then, tell her she's done so."

"Mr. Wheaton?"

"Well," Vince said, "I know our last card might have been a bit harsh. You see, it was a novelty card with some naked bodies—oh my. I see where she might have thought . . ."

"Do you agree with your wife?"

"Yes, yes, of course," Vince said. "Tell Robin we won't . . . bother her anymore."

"No more cards?"

"Certainly not," Amy said. "We only send greeting cards to our friends. You've made it abundantly clear that our circle of friends no longer includes Robin Lobianco."

"That's good then," Jones said. "I'll be going now . . . and I hope I won't have to come back here."

"I'll walk you out," Amy said, ignoring his remark. It was obvious that she was angry, but that didn't keep her hips from swaying while he followed her out. Actually, he figured she had no control over them.

At the door he said, "Can I ask you something?"

"Why not?" she asked. "You couldn't insult us any more than you already have."

Jones couldn't help but notice that the nipples of her bra-less breasts were hard beneath her T-shirt. Was this whole situation turning her on?

"Why send her greeting cards in the first place?"

"Just to let her know," Amy said, looking directly into Jones' eyes, "that we've been thinking about her."

After Jones left, Amy returned from walking him to the door and reclaimed her barstool.

"What a buffoon," Vince said. "Did he really think he was scaring us?"

"She called the police, Vince," Amy said, frowning. "She shouldn't have done that."

"Now, now, sugar," Vince said, "we haven't done anything the police can act against us for. No phone calls, no mail, nothing."

Amy kept tapping her glass with a nail.

"We'll have to talk to her," she said.

"Definitely," Vince said, "but how. Now that she's called the police she's introduced another element into the mix."

"Where's that invitation we got a few weeks ago?"

"Which one?" Vince asked.

"The one to that art exhibit," Amy said. "I think I put it in the desk drawer."

She walked to a small writing desk against the opposite wall and opened the top drawer.

"Yes, here it is." She carried it back to the bar and put it down in front of him.

"Oh, that one. That's downtown, isn't it? Not at the museum?" he asked.

"Maybe it's not at the Art Museum," she replied, "but I know Robin will be there."

"And so will we," Vince said. He leaned across the bar and kissed Amy on the cheek. "You're brilliant."

"I know."

"And incredibly sexy." He reached out and touched her nipple through the T-shirt.

"I know that, too," she purred.

"The big bad policeman couldn't take his eyes off you," he said, taking it between his thumb and forefinger now, and rolling it. "Did he get you excited?"

"Well, actually," she said, "he did."

"You like that type?" he asked. "He was like a . . . a big bear."

"He'd be rough, I think," she said.

He closed his hand over her breast now, squeezing cruelly. She caught her breath.

"You want it rough?" he demanded.

She smiled at him sweetly and said, "I thought you'd never ask, lover."

FIFTEEN

When Jones arrived home that night he was in possession of his Robin Lobianco file, and all the research material one of the computer geniuses in the department had come up with on Vincent and Amy Wheaton.

"Why are you taking such an interest in this case?" Katy asked him over a take-out dinner. "Is the woman that attractive?"

"You know better than that, Katy," he said. "How can I look at other women when I'm married to you?"

"Good answer," she said, "but it doesn't answer my question. And when are they going to give you a new partner? I don't like the idea of you running around alone out there without backup."

"Who knows when they'll assign me a new partner? Probably when they find someone foolish enough to volunteer."

She put her fork down and said, "It's not your fault your last three partners died."

"One died," he said, "two were killed."

"Same thing."

"Not to a cop."

"So they hand you cases like this one, where you have to make something out of it yourself?"

"I'm not making something out of it," he said.

"Then what is it?"

"The Wheatons are too slick, Katy," he said.

"You mean they're snobs, don't you?" she asked. "Had their noses in the air? You *hate* that."

"Yes, I do," he said, "but that wasn't it, either. Look, I'm just going to read over the research tonight and see what I can come up with on them."

"To scare them off?"

"I get the impression that these two won't scare easily," he said.

"What are they like?"

"Both beautiful people, real calm and collected . . . but she's in control."

"How can you tell?"

"They would look at each other before answering each question."

"So?"

"Later I realize that he was looking to her for approval, or for the answer," Jones said. "This woman controls her man."

"Don't all women?" she asked. "Don't I control you?"

He hoped that she hadn't said that even half kiddingly. The fact was she did control him, but only because he was obsessed with her and would do anything and give her anything to keep her. Part of the obsession was sexual, of course. Here he was a middle-aged cop without bright prospects for the future and he was married to and sleeping with a beautiful stripper. Wasn't that every middle-aged—or any aged—man's dream?

"Yes, dear, you do," he said, "but only because you have a golden pussy."

"And what about these?" she asked saucily, sliding her hands beneath her full breasts to cup and lift them. She was wearing a T-shirt and he could see that her nipples were hard and looked like big grapes beneath the shirt.

He eyed her critically and then said, "You might be right about those."

She looked down at her chest and said, "What do you mean?"

"You just might need new implants."

The phone rang at that moment and he rose quickly to get it before she threw her fork at him.

Literally saved by the bell.

When he got off the phone she asked, "Who was that?"

"The dispatcher," he said. "Seems Robin Lobianco called, wanting to talk to me."

"I hope they told her you were off duty."

"They did," he said, "but they also said they'd relay her message to me."

"What message?"

"Seems she got some phone calls."

"What kind?"

"Hang ups."

"We all get that," Katy said. "No reason to call the police."

Jones chewed the inside of his cheek thoughtfully and said, "Maybe I'd better take a run out there."

"Out where?"

"To her home."

"Where's that?"

"Out in South County, somewhere off of Gravois."

"South County?"

Jones and Katy had a small house in the Webster Groves section of town. It was an area she wanted to live in, and it had taken some time to find a house small enough and cheap enough for them to afford.

"So you're going?"

"She's frightened," he said, pulling on a windbreaker and clipping his holster to his belt. "I'll just go and settle her down and be right back."

She walked him to the door and said, "I've got to meet this woman, see her for myself."

"Why?"

"So I know whether or not to be jealous."

He pulled her to him, kissed her soundly and said, "Not."

But she watched him walk to his car, not so easily convinced.

When Robin opened the door Detective Jones thought she looked frightened. The look eased when she saw him.

"Thank you so much for coming over," she said.

"That's okay," he answered. "It kept my wife from killing me."

"Oh," she said, "you're married."

"Yes."

"I'm sorry, I dragged you away—"

"It's my job, Robin," he said. "She understands that."

"I'd be upset if my husband was called out to work in the evening," Robin said, "especially by another woman."

"You're not planning on seducing me, are you?" he asked.

"No! Of course n—"

"I'm sorry," he said. "In light of your problem that was probably in poor taste."

"Unless you consider offering you coffee and cake seduction," she added, playing along to put him at ease.

"No," he said, "but if you'd said coffee and donuts . . . to a cop, *that's* seduction."

Katy turned off the TV and went upstairs to dress for work. She was still thinking about Jack and the Lobianco woman. Was there an attraction there? She knew her husband was no Stone Philips, but he was a real man, and that attracted women. It was what had attracted her to him. He'd come into the club with a few cop friends and she'd been able to see immediately that he was out of place. The others were whooping it up, grabbing at the girls, waving dollar bills. Jack Jones was one of the few men she'd ever seen come into the club and actually eat something from the buffet.

That was when she knew she had to get to know him better. So it wasn't so far-fetched that another woman would find him appealing.

She had to come up with a plan to meet Robin Lobianco.

SIXTEEN

She played the message tape for him. Just hang ups, maybe a breath or two. He suggested she erase it.

"Why?"

"Because if you don't you'll keep playing it."

"Why would I do that?"

"I don't know the psychology behind it, Robin," he said, "but take my word for it. You will."

"Can't you trace it?"

"It's an incoming call and it's on tape," he said. "I could probably check the Wheatons' phone line but if it wasn't made from there, or if it wasn't a long distance call, we're out of luck. And they seem too smart to use their own phone, where there'd be a record."

She stared at the machine for a few seconds, then pressed the button to erase the tape.

"There you go," he said. "Now how about that cake?"

Over coffee and cake they talked a while. Not necessarily about her case, but about anything. After a while she realized that she'd been babbling about her life and her job and he hadn't said a thing about himself.

"You're a good listener," she said.

"That's my job."

"I'll bet you're a good detective."

"You'd get some argument about that from my bosses."

"Why?"

Now that the subject had gotten around to him he fidgeted uncomfortably.

"They think I'm a loose cannon," he said. "Some think I'm a jinx. They think that I have little or no respect for authority."

"And do you?"

"Sure," he said, "it's stupidity I have no respect for."

"And where do you find that prevalent?" she asked.

"Mostly in people who are in authority."

She wanted to talk more about him, but he stood up and said, "I'd better get going."

"Yes," she said, standing also, "your wife will be worried."

They walked into the living room together.

"We didn't talk much about my case, did we?" she asked.

"No, we didn't."

"You did that on purpose, didn't you?"

"What?"

"You let me talk on and on about everything that's of no interest to you, just so I wouldn't think about . . . my problem."

"You need somebody to talk to," he said. "Do you have a friend you can talk to?"

"Yes," she said, "her name is Brenda. She'd like you . . . uh, if you weren't married, that is. Well, no, Brenda wouldn't care, really, as long as I—" She stopped short and bit her lip. "I'm doing it again."

"Do you talk to her about this?"

"Except for you she's the only one I talk to about it."

"And does she advise you?"

Robin rolled her eyes. "Brenda is chock full of advice."

"Any of it good?"

"A lot of it, actually."

"Well," he said, "I'm glad you have a friend to talk to."

"Actually," she said, "I kind of feel like I have two." She put her hand on his arm. "Thank you."

"Don't mention it," he said. "I'll talk to you soon."

Before she could respond there was a knock on her door. She was shocked that a simple thing like that could suddenly make her feel frightened.

"They wouldn't," she said, in a whisper. "Would they?"

He knew it didn't take a key to get into the building because he'd gotten in without one.

"Okay, just relax," he said. "I'll answer it."

He walked to the door and looked through the peephole. He saw the distorted face of a man who was not Vince Wheaton, and then realized that Robin could do the same thing.

"Know this guy?" he asked.

She moved warily to the door and looked through the hole as though she thought it might bite her.

"It's Frank," she said, relief plain in her voice.

"Frank."

"My husband."

"Oh."

"My God," she said, with a new kind of fear, "what will I tell him?"

"We'll just say I'm here talking to you about some thefts from the museum, okay?"

"I'm a terrible liar," she said, worriedly.

"Then I'll lie and you nod."

"Okay."

Frank started to knock again just as Jones opened the door. When Robin saw the two men next to each other like that she realized why she found Jones appealing. They were both best described as "rumpled" looking, though Jones was a larger man.

Frank looked perplexed.

"Wha—who are you?" Before Jones could answer he directed the same question at Robin. "Who's this guy?"

Before Robin could answer Jones did.

"My name's Detective Jones, Mr. . . . Lobianco, is it?'

"That's right," Frank said, almost belligerently. "I'm her husband."

"I see," Jones said.

"What's a detective doing here?" Frank asked, again directing the question to Robin.

"We uh—" Robin said, but Jones cut her off.

"I'm investigating a report of some thefts from the museum," Jones said.

"This isn't the museum."

Jones smiled tolerantly and said, "I've been to the museum, I just had some additional questions to ask Mrs. Lobianco."

"This late at night?"

"I called first."

"And I told him to come over," Robin chimed in.

Jones turned toward Robin now and pointedly ignored the husband.

"Thank you for your time, Mrs. Lobianco. I'll be in touch with you about my findings."

"Why her?" Frank asked.

"Sorry?"

"Why get in touch with her?" Frank asked. "Why not her boss."

"Mrs. Lobianco is the one who called the police," Jones said. "She is my contact at the museum. Is that a problem, sir?"

Frank hesitated, then said, "Uh, no, I guess not . . ."

"Then I'll say thank you again," Jones said, "and bid you both good-night."

"Good-night, detective," Robin said, "and thank you."

Jones nodded and left. Frank watched him walk down the hall until he disappeared down the steps, and then moved to step inside the apartment.

"What are you doing here, Frank?" she demanded, putting her hand on his chest to stop him.

"I haven't heard from you in a week," Frank said. "I thought we had a good dinner last week and you haven't called or answered my calls since then."

"We did have a nice dinner," she said, "but does that mean we have to talk every day? Or every week?"

"You're my wife, Robin."

"And we're separated, Frank," she said. "That means we're supposed to be seeing how we can live without each other."

"Well, I can't," he said. "At least, I can't live without hearing from you, that you're all right. I call and call—"

"I think you're exaggerating, Frank," she said. "I think I had one message from you at work and one at home—wait a minute. Did you call here today?"

"What? No, why?"

"You didn't call and hang up without leaving a message?"

"No," he said, "why would I do that? Have you been getting hang up calls?"

"Just a few—"

"Obscene calls?" he asked, concerned. "Is that why the detective was here?"

"Detective Jones told you why he was here, Frank," she said, "and it wasn't because of obscene calls."

"Robin, if you want I could stay—"

"I'm tired, Frank," she said, "I want to go to bed . . . to sleep."

He looked so wounded that she reached out and stroked his face with her right hand.

"You're sweet to be worried, Frank, but I'm fine. Really."

"Will you call me tomorrow?" he asked. "Just so I don't worry?"

"I will," she said. "I promise."

She dropped her hand and he hesitated. She hoped he wouldn't start in on her right then and there about coming home.

"All right," he said, grudgingly. "Good-night, then."

"Good-night, Frank."

It was her turn to watch him until he disappeared down the steps, and then she went back inside and closed her door.

Outside Vince and Amy Wheaton watched from a car across the parking lot. They saw the arrival and departure of Detective Jones, and then the same coming and going of Frank Lobianco.

"That damn detective," Vince said, from behind the driver's seat. They were not in their Lexus, which Robin had seen many times now, but a nondescript Chrysler.

Amy reached out and took her husband's hand.

"Don't worry, love," she said. "We're smarter than he is."

"Much smarter."

"Besides, he's not going to devote all that much time to this," she said. "He's got bigger fish to fry."

"Unless she's sleeping with him, the bitch."

Now she rubbed his hand and said, "Don't get jealous, she's not sleeping with him. He's just a policeman. She probably called him after she heard our hang ups on her phone machine."

"Okay," he said, "I won't be jealous of the cop, but what about the husband?"

Amy leaned her head back.

"I've been thinking about him," she said. "She became very agitated at Duff's when I told her she didn't want him."

"Maybe you're wrong."

"And maybe we need to have him out of the way," Amy said, "so she can make her final decision."

Vince smiled and said, "Maybe."

SEVENTEEN

The first call that morning came to Robin, as she was dressing for work. She hesitated then decided to go ahead and answer the phone.

"Robin Lobianco?" a man's voice asked.

"Y-yes?" It didn't sound like Vince Wheaton. "Who's this?"

"My name is Detective Winston. We, uh, have your husband in St. John's hospital, Ma'am."

"My husband? For what?"

"Well . . ."

The second call came to Jack Jones' house. He had awakened spooned up against his wife's tight little naked butt and his dick had begun to creep up the crack in her ass when the phone rang.

"Jack," she moaned.

"I'll get rid of them," he promised, and reached across her to answer it.

First mistake of the day.

"Why would anyone want to hurt Frank?" Robin asked.

Jones looked over at her in the passenger seat of his Taurus. He'd decided to pick her up rather than have her drive to Sunset Hills herself to meet him at the hospital.

"Did they say exactly what happened?"

"No," she said, "only that he'd been . . . attacked."

"Was your husband doing anything—I mean, was he into anything illegal—"

"He wouldn't do anything illegal!" she insisted.

"—then maybe he was just the victim of a mugging."

"I don't know," she said. "They were so vague on the phone. Why do cops have to be so vague?"

He shrugged and said, "I don't know," not offering any argument.

Jones shook his head. He didn't know what it was about this woman that made him want to help her. It certainly wasn't a sexual attraction—something he'd tried to explain to Katy that morning as he'd gotten dressed . . .

"Come on, Jack," she said. "There's only one reason a man wants to help a pretty woman—and you said she's pretty."

"Not as pretty as you," he said, looking around for his gun and holster. He spotted it on the nightstand, grabbed it and clipped it to his belt. Then he looked at her, still in bed, still naked but beneath the sheet—which clung to her every curve so that she might as well have been naked.

"Katy, she just needs help, that's all."

"Why do you have to be the one to help her?"

"Because I'm the one she called."

Katy frowned.

"Maybe I don't have to worry about you being attracted to her," she said. "Maybe it's the other way around."

He doubted that very much. She just didn't know who else to reach out to. When she'd asked him on the phone if he could "please" help her he'd been unable to say no.

"You're not really worried about that, are you?"

"Just go, Jack," she said. "If you're going . . . go."

"My very own boy scout," Katy had called after him as he'd left and maybe she was right.

"Well," he said to Robin, "I guess we'll get all the answers to our questions when we get there."

She folded her arms across her breasts and said, "God, I hope so . . ."

EIGHTEEN

At the hospital Jones and Robin were greeted by Detective Dan Winston, who worked on the same squad as Jones.

"Jack," Winston said, surprised, "what are you doing here?"

"Mrs. Lobianco called me," Jones said. "I'm working a case that might be related."

Winston stared at Jones and Robin. Winston had never been called in an emergency by anyone connected to any case he was working on. Winston was Jones' age, overweight and balding and living with a wife who had gotten a face-lift, a tummy tuck, and a butt lift, to little or no avail. He couldn't figure out what a stripper would see in Jones. Now here he was showing up at the hospital with another younger woman. What did the guy have that he didn't?

"This one's my case," he told Jones.

"I'm not looking to take your case, Dan," Jones said, "but Mrs. Lobianco would like to know what's going on, and I'm also curious about why Major Case would be called in on this. Was it something more than a mugging?"

"We're not sure what it is, Jack—Mrs. Lobianco, can I speak to you in private?"

"I'd prefer to have Detective Jones present," she said, "if you don't mind."

Winston obviously did mind but he said, "It's up to you. Ma'am, your husband was found in a section of Forest Park, beaten and unconscious, and brought here."

"How was he I.D.'d?" Jones asked.

"He still had his wallet."

"And cash?"

Winston gave Jones an annoyed look and said, "Lots of cash. Look, Jack, can we talk in private for a minute?"

"Why don't you get a doctor to talk to Mrs. Lobianco about her husband's condition," Jones suggested, "and then you and I can talk."

"Fine. Wait here."

"I don't understand," Robin said.

"You might have been better off coming without me."

"Does that man have something against you? He seems very angry that you're here."

"It's a long story."

"I'd like you to stay, if you would."

Jones hesitated then said, "All right."

Winston returned with the attending physician, who took Robin to a small lounge to talk with her.

"Okay, Dan," Jones said, "let's have it."

"I'm going to call the office and have you pulled, Jack. I don't want you here."

"I'm not here officially," Jones said, "so I can't be pulled. I'm only here at Mrs. Lobianco's request."

"Does your wife know about Mrs. Lobianco?"

"Everything," Jones said, tightly. "She was home when I took the call. You got something else you want to say?"

"Don't get in my way, Jack."

"I try never to get in anyone's way, Dan."

"Tell that to your ex-partner's widows."

Jones might have swung at Winston if Robin had not returned at that moment.

"How is he?" Jones asked.

"The doctor says he'll recover," she said. "His injuries aren't life threatening. He has a concussion, possibly a broken rib, and lots of bruises." She turned to look at Winston. "Now that I've talked to the doctor maybe you'll tell me why you're here, Detective, when it looks to me like it's my husband who is the victim?"

"Well, Ma'am," Winston said. "We found several items of interest to us on your husband's person."

"On his person?" she asked, openly annoyed. "What exactly do you mean by 'on his person,' Detective? Do you mean in his pocket or tattooed on his forehead?"

Winston looked at Jones, as if for help, but all he got back was a blank stare. Your case, Jones thought.

"Ma'am," Winston said, "there's no need to get upset—"

"Then why don't you tell me what this is about, Detective?" she asked. "Maybe then there will be a need."

"We found condoms in one of his pockets," Winston said, "and drugs in another."

"Drugs? What kind of drugs?"

"We sent it in to be analyzed, but we believe it was crack cocaine."

Robin looked at Jones.

"Frank has never used drugs in his life, except for some marijuana," she said. "Something is wrong, here."

"What are you assuming, Dan?" Jones asked. "I mean, from the crack and from the condoms."

"He was found in a section of the park that is known for homosexual activity," Winston said. "We're thinking maybe he went there to . . . meet somebody to, uh, have sex and maybe to sell some drugs."

"That's craz—" Robin started, but Jones put his hand on her arm.

"So whoever he met with beat him up and then left him lying there with his wallet and crack in his pockets?"

"They might have been scared away," Winston said.

"What does Mr. Lobianco say?" Jones asked.

"What else would he say?" Winston asked. "He doesn't know how he got there. He says he went to see his wife, spoke with her, and then went right home. He remembers putting the key into his door lock and that's it. Next thing he knows he's here in the emergency room."

"That's fine," Winston said, "but can you vouch for the fact that he wasn't there to meet someone, or to sell drugs?"

"My husband is not gay," Robin said, "I can certainly vouch for that. As for him using or selling drugs, that's just ridiculous."

"Well, Ma'am," Winston said, "what I'm going to do is investigate and find out whether or not it is ridiculous. That's my job. Will you excuse me a moment? I have to make a call."

As Winston walked away Robin asked, "Who is he calling?"

"Probably our boss," Jones said, "to get me removed from here."

"Can he do that?"

"If my boss tells me to leave I'll have to leave, or get into trouble," he explained.

"God," she said, "I didn't mean to get you in trouble."

"Why don't we wait and see what happens. Meanwhile, can you get in to see your husband?"

"The doctor says yes," she said, "as long as it's all right with the police."

"Well," Jones said, taking hold of her elbow, "I'm the police. While Winston is on the phone let's go and tell the doctor it's all right."

NINETEEN

Jones stood outside Frank Lobianco's room while Robin was inside talking to him. After a few moments Detective Winston came storming down the hall.

"What the hell do you think you're doing?" he demanded. "She can't talk to him until I say so."

"Oops," Jones said, with no expression on his face.

Winston stood there speechless for a moment.

"Talk to the boss?" Jones asked.

"No," Winston said, tightly. "Couldn't get him."

"If you'll loosen up, Dan, I'll be out of here in no time," Jones said. "You can go after Lobianco all you want. I don't care. I'm just here as a favor to Mrs. Lobianco."

"What's your relationship with her, anyway?"

"I told you," Jones replied. "I'm working on a case she's involved in. She called me when you called her."

"What about your wife—"

"If you try to make something out of this that it's not," Jones warned, "they're going to have to give you a room here."

The two glared at each other, one belligerently and the other—Jones—with no expression. The door to the room opened and Robin stepped out.

"Do you need Mrs. Lobianco anymore?" Jones asked.

"I'll need a statement—"

"She'll come down and make one later," Jones said. "Anything else?"

Winston compressed his lips, then said, "No. That's all."

"You ready to leave?" Jones asked Robin.

"Yes," she said, wearily. "I—there's nothing else I can do here."

"Dan," Jones said, "she'll come to the office and make that statement later. I'll see you there, as well."

"You'll see me in the boss's office," Winston said, angrily.

"That's fine," Jones said. "Maybe I'll take that opportunity to request you as a partner."

Winston was sputtering as Jones and Robin went down the hall.

Outside the hospital Jones asked, "Are you going to work?"

"I called in this morning and took the day off," she said. "I . . . didn't know how long this would take."

"Let's go someplace and talk about your case," he said. "I've been doing some research."

"All right," she said. "Actually, I'm pretty hungry."

"Let's find an Einstein's Bagels or something." He took her arm and directed her towards his car.

They found a generic bagel place and sat down by the window with coffee, a blueberry for her and a poppy seed for him. Both eschewed cream cheese and just took butter.

"Are you all right?" he asked.

"Yes, I'm . . . confused, but all right."

"What did Frank say?"

"The same thing he told the other detective," she answered. "He doesn't know what happened."

"Robin," he said, warily, "don't get angry at me, okay? I have to ask these questions."

She closed her eyes. "I know what you're going to ask, but okay."

"You never had any indication that Frank was using drugs?"

"No."

"Or selling them?"

"No." She was adamant.

"Couldn't he have become involved in that since your separation?"

She opened her mouth, then closed it, thought a moment and then shrugged.

"I suppose it's possible," she said. "But everything I know about Frank says no. He's a decent man, Detective."

"Look," he said, "if you're going to start calling me in the middle of the night for favors I think you better call me Jack."

"It wasn't the middle—I get your point . . . Jack."

"Good," Jones said. "What about the gay thing?"

"Believe me, I can attest to the fact that Frank isn't gay."

"Your sex life was always good?"

"Well . . . no . . ."

"There were problems?"

"Just some problems of compatibility," she said. "I mean, he likes it at night, I like it in the morning, we like . . . different positions . . . that sort of thing. Don't most couples go through that?"

Jones didn't know. He'd been a bachelor his whole life. Katy was his first wife, and they screwed everywhere they could and in every position. His only problem was trying to keep up with her.

"I suppose so."

"You and your wife—"

"No," he said, "no problem."

"Well . . ." she said, ". . . good for you."

"You'll have to come to the office and make a statement."

"All right," she said. "Will you try to prove Frank innocent?"

Jones took a few moments to form his response.

"Robin, I can't work on his case," he said. "It belongs to Winston."

"But . . . but that man will only try to prove him guilty."

"Winston's an asshole," Jones said, "but he'll do his job."

"But you—"

"I tell you what," he said. "I'll continue to work it from your side, and maybe I'll come across something that will help."

She stared at him a moment.

"Are you saying you think Vince and Amy had something to do with this?"

He wasn't saying that, he was just trying to tell her something that would appease her, but what if they did have something to do with it?

"Robin, was there any chance that you and Frank would get back together?"

"Well, there was always a chance . . ."

"What if Vince and Amy knew that?" he asked. "What if they thought getting him out of the way would affect your decision?"

"You mean they tried to kill him so I'd move in with them?" she asked. "That sounds crazy."

"You told me you thought they were crazy."

"Yes, but—"

"And they didn't try to kill him," Jones said, cutting her off. "It seems to me they're trying to discredit him in your eyes, so that you won't go back to him."

"Trying to make me think he sells drugs and is . . . is gay? Why wouldn't they take his picture with a woman and show it to me? Wouldn't that have been less trouble?"

"You've had sex since your separation."

"Well, yes . . . once."

"Would you hold it against Frank if he did?"

"I don't—well, I guess he could, but—"

"Maybe it seemed to them that there was more chance you'd hold it against him that he was a gay drug dealer."

She put her hand to her forehead and said, "God, this all sounds so melodramatic, like a bad movie."

"I know," he said. "Life is like that sometimes—from my point of view, anyway."

"But not mine," she said. "My life is supposed to be normal. Jesus, why did I ever . . . do this in the first place?"

"Maybe you weren't so happy being normal?" Jones said.

"Maybe not," she said, "but if I could go back—"

"There's no use in thinking that way," he said. "Look, let me tell you about some of this research I've done."

"All right."

"Stalking laws differ from state to state," he said, "but they can be arrested for it if I have probable cause to believe that they're a threat to you."

"Well, after this—"

"We don't know they did this to Frank," he reminded her, "and you haven't told me that you fear for your safety."

"If I tell you that will you arrest them?"

"I could," he said, "but I doubt they'd be held for very long, and they don't seem like the kind of people who would be frightened by being arrested."

"Then what—"

"You'd end up in court with them and would have to prove they were stalking you, and were a danger to you."

"And then we're back to me telling the whole story in court," she said.

She closed her hands into fists and he could tell this was something she was not used to doing.

"If I knew that they had done this to Frank then it would be worth . . . exposing myself to that."

"That's fair," he said. "We can wait a while and see what Winston . . . and I . . . come up with."

"So you will work on it?"

"I'll . . . see what I can do."

She reached across the table and took his hand. A wave of emotion came over him, and he realized it wasn't sexual. He just wanted to make it better for her. Jesus, he thought, is this feeling . . . am I feeling fatherly toward her?

"Why are you being so kind to me?" she asked. "Are you this way with all your cases?"

"No," he said, easing his hand from hers, "I'm not, and I'm not sure I can answer your question. Just be grateful that I caught your case instead of Dan Winston."

"Oh," she said, eyes widening, "I am. Believe me, I am."

TWENTY

"What is it about this woman that makes you want to help her?" Katy Jones asked her husband.

"I'm not sure," he said.

"Do you want to fuck her, Jack?"

"What—God, no, Katy. It's not that. It's . . ."

"It's what?"

He looked up at her, standing over him in their living room. She was getting ready to leave for work when the subject of Robin Lobianco came up, and now she was demanding an explanation.

"Come on, Jack," she said. "You're going above and beyond your duty here. If you've got a thing for this girl I'd like to know—"

"I think," he said, cutting her off, "I'm feeling . . . protective of her."

"Protective?"

"Yes," he said, "like . . . like a father."

She stared at him, amazed.

"That's either the dumbest excuse, or—how old is she?"

"I don't know," he said, "about twenty-eight, maybe thirty."

"She's older than me."

"Yes."

"Well, you don't feel paternal towards me," Katy said, "why her?"

Jones looked at his wife. She was wearing a T-shirt with no bra and her breasts were straining the fabric. Her jeans were so tight he could see the outline of her panties underneath. How could any man look at her and feel anything remotely paternal.

Robin Lobianco was a different story, though. In spite of the fact that she admitted to a ménage à trois with the Wheatons she simply did not strike Jones as being wild, or even worldly. She was a Midwest girl who got caught up in something exciting for a while, but now she needed help getting out of it.

"You don't need a father, Katy."

"Well, you got that right!" He knew all about her problems with her own father, which caused her to believe that fatherhood—and motherhood, by association—were highly overrated.

"Well, this girl needs somebody," he said. "I don't know if it's a father, maybe it's a friend. She's mixed up in something she can't handle."

"Did it ever occur to you that she might be playing you?" Katy asked. "That maybe she and her husband have been selling drugs?"

"No."

"No what?"

"No, she's not playing me," he said. "Maybe I've slipped, but I'm not that bad."

Suddenly, Katy's entire demeanor changed. She dropped to her knees in front of him and took his hands.

"Oh, sweetie," she said, "you haven't slipped. Don't talk like that. You're as good a cop as you ever were. You've had a streak of bad luck lately, that's all."

"Well," he said, holding her hands tightly, "I did one thing right that I know of."

"Oh yeah," she said, "you married a stripper. That really put you in good with the department."

She hugged him then, her full breasts pressed against his chest. Paternal feelings were the furthest thing from his mind.

"I've got an idea," she said.

"What?"

"I'll invite her to dinner."

He stared at her.

"You're going to cook?"

"No, silly," she said, "I'll invite her to go out with us for dinner."

"I don't think that's a good idea, Katy."

"Why not?" she asked. "Don't you want me to meet her?"

"That's not it," he said. "She already had dinner with a couple and now they're stalking her. I mean, there's more to it than that, but—"

"Okay," she said, "I see your point. What if I call her and invite her to lunch with me?"

"I think that would be a great idea."

"You do?" She had half expected him to veto that idea, too.

"Yes, I do. Go ahead and do it. I'll leave the number for you."

"Okay, I will." She stood up. "I've got to go to work."

"Be careful."

"Always. I'm sorry about how I've been acting about this girl, but . . . if she really is in need of help she's come to the right guy."

"Thanks, babe."

"But you can't blame me for feeling just a little bit jealous."

"I kind of like it," he said. "Makes this middle-aged man feel good."

"We'll see how middle-aged you are when I get home," she said. "I'll wake you."

"Make sure you do."

"If I can, that is," she said, walking out the door. "You know how soundly you old-timers sleep."

The door closed behind her before he could get off a parting shot.

TWENTY-ONE

Katy wasted no time and called Robin Lobianco the next day. She invited her to lunch and was surprised when the other woman readily accepted. They agreed that Katy would come to the Art Museum and they would lunch there.

"You're staring," Katy said, when they were seated. "Tell me you've never seen a real live stripper before."

Robin blushed and looked away, embarrassed that she'd been caught.

Katy had gone straight to her office rather than meet at the restaurant so there'd be no problem recognizing one another. All they'd done while walking from Robin's office to the restaurant was "nice to meet you" and "nice to meet you." Now, as they were seated, Katy caught Robin looking.

"I'm sorry . . ." Robin said.

"It's okay," Katy said, with a smile. "Most women are curious about strippers—how we can do it? Why do we do it?"

"I would never ask—"

"It's simple," Katy said. "I make a living. I'm not the brightest woman in the world, but I do have a good body and I can make a living showing it off. It doesn't mean I make porn movies, or that I'm a prostitute. I'm not one of those bimbos you see on Jerry Springer."

"I can't believe you're not bright," Robin said. "You seem very smart, and I don't think Detective Jones would marry a woman who wasn't."

"First," Katy said, her hackles rising, "I didn't say I wasn't bright, I simply said I wasn't the 'brightest' woman around. I'm smart, but it's in ways you don't learn in school. You went to college, didn't you?"

"Of course, but—"

"Why do people who went to college always answer that question with 'of course.' I never went to college, I had to go out and make a living on my own."

"I'm sorry," Robin said. "I didn't mean to offend you. I think we're getting off on the wrong foot . . ."

"No, no," Katy insisted, "we're fine. I guess maybe I am a little thin-skinned about what I do for a living, and my education. It's fine. What's good here?"

That night when Jones came home he asked Katy how the lunch went.

"Well," she said, "I can see why you like her. She's smart and pretty. I can also see why you want to help her. She does come off as a victim, doesn't she?"

"Oh, I don't know—"

"All right," Katy said, "then as the type who needs somebody to help her."

"Well . . ."

"In any case," she went on, "you don't have to worry about me being jealous."

"Oh? Why not?"

"She's not your type."

"Is that a fact?"

"Oh yes, it is," Katy said.

"And what is it about her that makes her not my type?"

"She's not strong enough to be your type," Katy said. "Although if you were with her you'd be so busy taking care of her that you wouldn't notice your own problems."

Jones stared at Katy for a few moments, then said, "You didn't like her, did you?"

"Not at all."

"Why not?"

"Because she's bright, and educated, and has a snooty job—she's the exact opposite of me, except for the fact that she's got big boobs. You know, I could probably make a stripper out of her."

"Her being smart doesn't make her the opposite of you," Jones said. "I'd stack your smarts up against any college educated woman's."

"Oh, don't get me wrong," Katy said. "I don't envy her the college education and the job. It's just that she's so uptight, and has no idea what the real world is like. Maybe this whole stalking thing is just what she needs to smarten her up."

"No woman needs to be stalked," Jones said.

"No, but sometimes a man does," she teased, sliding her arms around him.

"You didn't stalk me," he said, "you pursued me until you caught me."

"No," she said, "I pursued you until you caught me."

He hugged her tightly and then she said, "I feel like a game."

He slid his hand down her back until he was caressing her butt.

"You know," she said, as they walked toward the stairs with their arms around each other, "having met her, I can't believe that girl ever took part in a ménage à trois."

"I think part of the problem is," he said, "neither can she."

TWENTY-TWO

Jack Jones found out several things about the Wheatons over the weekend and into the following week.

"They don't own the house they're living in," he told Katy over breakfast on Wednesday. He was using her as a sounding board these days, since none of the detectives on his squad wanted to be around him. It was good for them, though. She felt a part of his work, and he talked to her about Robin Lobianco, which eased any thoughts she might have had that he was having an affair with her.

"Are they renting?"

"Sub-letting," he said. "Apparently they've only been living there for about five months."

"Where did they live before that?"

"Don't know," he said. "I'm still trying to find out."

"How did they find out about the sub-let being available?"

"I don't know that, either."

"Well then," she suggested, "maybe you should check with some of the high-scale realtors in town. A house in that neighborhood wouldn't be listed with just anybody."

"You're a pretty smart girl."

"I'm a cop's wife," she said. "Some parts of the life rub off . . . maybe while we're rubbing parts."

"You're a dirty girl."

"I know," she said. "Here's something else I know."

"What's that?"

"We haven't played any games since this whole stalking thing started."

"My fault," he said.

"Maybe tonight?" she asked. "Farmer's Daughter?"

He raised his eyebrows. Farmer's Daughter always wore him out.

"Maybe," he said. "We'll see."

"Okay, then," she said, "what else have you found out about these wonderful Wheatons?"

"They don't have Missouri driver's licenses."

"So they're either driving around without a license," she surmised, or they haven't gotten around to changing them."

"Right."

"What about their car?"

"Not registered here," he said. "They must have out-of-state plates."

"So if you find out what state the plates are from, you can check them out there," she said.

"That's just what I'm going to do today," he said. "I.D. their plates. Robin never noticed them. Once I have a number I'll run it."

"And I'm going to go grocery shopping."

He watched her as she cleared the table. They'd been married two years and he had still never been grocery shopping with her. He wondered what she wore to the store? At the moment she was wearing what she usually wore in the house, even in the winter: T-shirt and cut-off jeans. He wondered if she changed before she went outside. They both worked such odd hours that most of the time they spent together was spent inside.

"Anything else interesting about them?" she asked.

"Well yeah," Jones said, "they don't work, apparently."

"Where do they get their money?"

"I don't know," he said, "but I'm going to find that out, too."

"Well, considering the house and neighborhood they're living in they certainly want people to think they have money," Katy said.

"And they must have *some,*" Jones said, "since they don't work."

"Maybe Robin knows where their money comes from," Katy suggested. "Have you asked her?"

"No, but I will . . . and I better get to it."

She walked with him towards the front door.

"Did Robin tell you about our lunch?"

"I haven't seen her since then."

"I'll be interested in her take on it."

"I'll let you know."

"What's happening with her husband's case?" she asked, as they reached the door.

"He's still in the hospital."

"What happens when the hospital releases him?"

"Robin wants to bail him out."

"How much?"

"Don't know," Jones said. "His arraignment has been put off until he's physically able to attend."

"How much do you think?"

"Not a lot," he said. "We're not talking about murder, here."

"That's good," she said. "I have to tell you something."

"What?"

"You've been different since you've been out there chasing these stalkers. I kind of like it. Does that make me awful?"

He pulled her to him and said, "Nothing makes you awful, babe. You're the only good thing in my life, right now."

"I'll always be good to you, Jack," she said, nuzzling him in the open doorway.

"Okay, quit it," he said, as her hand snaked down to his crotch, "the neighbors are watching."

"Let them watch," she said. "They're all jealous that you've got yourself a real live stripper, anyway."

He kissed her again, then slapped her butt and said, "Get your Farmer's Daughter outfit ready for tonight."

"I'll be waiting, tiger."

TWENTY-THREE

Wednesday morning Robin awoke and dressed for work. She was thinking about the art show that was to be held that night in a gallery on Grand Avenue, near the famed Fox Theater. Both she and Dance, as representatives of the St. Louis Art Museum, were supposed to attend. She didn't much feel like having drinks and mingling with the art lovers of St. Louis, but she didn't have much of a choice. She decided, however, to leave work early and return home to dress for the event. Dance would certainly not hold that against her, since he expected to see her there looking her best.

When she arrived at work she found a message on her desk that Dance wanted to see her. She wondered if he'd finally figured out a way to get her fired.

There was only one way to find out.

"Ah, come in, Mrs. Lobianco," Dance said, as she entered his office. "Take a seat, please. Can I get you something? Coffee? Tea?"

"No, sir," Robin said, sitting. She didn't think he'd be offering her refreshments if he was going to fire her.

"No? Well, then, I'll get right to the point. I've agreed to co-host the art show that we'll be attending tonight."

"Co-host?" she asked. "I thought we were attending as a courtesy."

"We were," he said, "but as of today we are co-hosting and deferring some of the cost."

And taking some credit, she thought. Robin knew

Caroline Webley, the woman who had worked very hard to put this show together in her private gallery. She wondered how William Dance had managed to get his dirty little fingers into her pie, so to speak.

"Well," she said, "that's nice."

"It's more than nice," he said. "It's important. That's why I want you to hostess it with Mrs. Webley."

"How does Caroline feel about that?"

"She's thrilled," Dance said. "I just wanted to call you in and let you know so that you'll be prepared. You'll have to look your best, you know."

"I'll certainly try, sir."

"Excellent," he said. "Then feel free to go home early in order to get dressed."

"Thank you, sir. Is that all?"

"That's all."

She stood up and started for the door.

"Oh, one more thing, Robin."

"Yes," she asked, turning as she reached the open doorway.

"This evening has to go off without a hitch," he said. "There'll be press coverage, print and—hopefully—television. Nothing must go wrong. Do you understand?"

"I understand," she said, "perfectly."

He'd managed to get the Art Museum some credit it didn't deserve, and had arranged it so that if anything went wrong it would be her fault.

He was so good at his job.

When she got back to her office she called Caroline Webley.

"How did Dance manage this?" she asked her.

"I'm not sure," Caroline said, "but I think he got to my

artist and convinced him that the show would be much more successful under the auspices of the Art Museum."

"Boy," Robin said, "Dance is a lot more than just his name. And you agreed to this?"

"Only under the condition that you co-host with me, and not him," Caroline replied.

"Ah," Robin said. He'd managed to make that sound like his idea, as well.

"Wear something slinky, dear," Caroline said. "There will be plenty of cameras."

"I don't do slinky very well, Caroline," Robin said. "It's not my style."

"Then wear something revealing," Caroline said, "and don't tell me you don't have the body for that. Remember, we've taken steam together."

"You're a hussy, Caroline."

"True, dear, very true," the other woman said. "See you tonight."

Robin hung up and the phone rang again immediately. She assumed it was either Caroline using speed dial to call back, or Dance calling her again.

"Hello?"

"Am I still invited to this big 'do' of yours tonight?" Brenda asked.

"Well, it wasn't my 'do,' but apparently it is now."

"Explain, please."

So Robin did, telling her friend about her conversation with both Dance and Caroline.

"Oh God," Brenda said, "so what do you suppose I should wear?"

Robin got an idea.

"Wear something slinky, Bren," she said. "At least you have the body for it."

"Something slinky," Brenda repeated. "I think I can manage that. What color are you wearing?"

"Red."

"Okay," she said, "I'll wear something slinky and stay away from red. I'm not bringing a date. Any eligible men attending?"

"Tons," Robin said, "and they're the rich kind."

"My hair," Brenda said, "I need to get my hair done. I have to get off the phone."

"Seven p.m., Brenda," Robin said, "sharp. I'll meet you outside. I want to walk in with you."

"We'll knock their socks off."

Robin hung up, starting to think that this might end up being fun.

TWENTY-FOUR

When Brenda showed up in front of the gallery Robin couldn't believe it.

"My God, girl," she said, as her friend approached her, "you're beautiful."

"Don't sound so surprised."

Robin wasn't surprised. She knew Brenda was attractive, but on this night she was a stunning vision in turquoise. She wore an ankle length gown that was cut low in front and—no doubt—in back, and around her shoulders she wore a pashmina of the same color. Her hair was done up and in her ears sparkled diamond earrings. Her make up, often overdone, was muted tonight, giving her a soft look that went with the color of the gown. In the end the look she achieved was—well, slinky, as well as sexy.

"Look at you," Brenda said. "You're not exactly dowdy."

The outfit Robin was wearing was more maroon than red. It was a dress, not a gown, and although her shoulders were covered the front was scooped out to show a deep, shadowy cleavage.

"Are you wearing that click bra?" Brenda asked.

"No," Robin said, "it's all me."

"Well," Brenda said, "I'm clicked up high in mine."

Robin suspected as much. While Brenda's skin was naturally pale and smooth, almost glowing, her cleavage did look a bit enhanced tonight. Brenda's only complaint about her own body was her smallish breasts, but she would never even consider implants. She'd heard too many horror stories about them and said that push-up bras were fine with her.

"Besides," she'd said once, "by the time a man has me out of my bra I've got him right where I want him."

Now Brenda looked inside the gallery window and said, "Where is everyone? Didn't you tell me it started at seven?"

"I told you to be here at seven," Robin said. "It starts at seven-thirty."

"You thought I'd be late?"

"Well, it's a quarter after seven."

"Okay, okay," Brenda said, "point taken."

"I have to get inside so I can meet and greet."

"Well," Brenda said, "I was hoping to make more of an entrance, but . . ."

Robin opened the door and Brenda followed her in. Caroline Webley spotted Robin right away and came gliding over. Caroline had the ability to look like she was gliding, and the white gown she was wearing certainly helped the illusion. She was blonde—though not as blonde as Brenda—and her hair combined with the gown made her look positively angelic—which Robin knew was far from the truth. Caroline was working on her fourth husband, and none of her divorces had been amicable. In fact, one of her husbands had tried to get "demonic possession" on the divorce papers as the cause.

"Robin, darling," Caroline said.

"You look lovely, Caroline," Robin said.

"So do you, dear," Caroline replied, "but who is your friend?"

"This is Brenda Telford, Carrie," Robin said. "You've heard me mention her."

"Oh, yes," Caroline said, coldly, "how do you do?" She promptly ignored Brenda and turned her attention to

Robin. The woman was apparently bitchy enough to be bothered by how good Brenda looked.

"The guests will be arriving soon."

"Should we greet them together?" Robin asked. "You have way more experience at this than I do."

"I think we can circulate separately," Caroline said. "I'll recognize most of them on sight, and I'll introduce you to the more important ones."

"All right." It was clear to Robin that Caroline wanted to get to "the most important ones" first.

Caroline patted Robin's arm and said, "The important thing is to have a good time. A little later on I'll introduce you to the artist."

"Fine."

Caroline gave Brenda a wan smile and walked away.

"What a bitch."

This was why Robin had never introduced Brenda and Caroline before. She knew they would not like each other. For some reason she got along fine with Caroline, but Brenda was another blonde, as classy looking as Caroline, but about ten years younger. Robin had to admit that of the two Brenda looked the best tonight, and that certainly did not sit well with Caroline.

"She's not so bad."

"Maybe not to you," Brenda said, "but I've got an icicle hanging from the tip of my nose."

"It's your own fault," Robin said, with mock severity.

"My fault? How do you figure that?"

Robin smiled this time and said, "You just look too damn good."

"Well," Brenda replied, "I can't help *that.*"

"Guests are starting to arrive," Robin said, looking past Brenda at the people who were filing in the door.

"Well, you go and play hostess," Brenda said. "I'm going to go and find the bar. Uh, it's not a cash bar, is it?"

"No," Robin said, "not a cash bar."

Brenda made a face and said, "Then I'll have to figure out another way to get a man's attention other than having him buy me a drink."

Robin looked her friend up and down and said, "Somehow I don't think that's going to be a problem for you tonight, Bren."

TWENTY-FIVE

The evening went well for a couple of hours. Robin met the artist, a young man with a very serious attitude about his work, which somehow involved showing a lot of skin without showing any nudity. It was a photographic art show, and he apparently had a way with cameras.

"I could do wonders with you," he told her when they met. She assumed he was talking about using a camera. "Let me introduce you to my friend Brenda," she replied, and that was that. Brenda and the artist disappeared for a little while.

Everything went well until Caroline approached her with a man and a woman to introduce them, but before she could get started the man said, "Oh, we're very well acquainted with Robin, aren't we, darling?"

Amy looked at Vince, smiled and said, "Oh yes, we certainly are, dear."

"Well then," Caroline said before a dumbstruck Robin could summon her voice, "I'll leave you to it."

"My God," Robin said, "you have nerve."

"Nerve?" Vince asked. "What do you mean?"

"You know what I mean." Robin fought to keep her voice down. This had all the potential of a catastrophe. Her boss had told her this had to go off without a hitch, and the last thing she needed now was a scene.

"The cards, the phone calls . . . Detective Jones talked to you about them."

"That was a very bad thing you did, Robin," Vince said, "calling the police. A very bad thing."

"It hurt our feelings," Amy said.

"We know you're confused, dear," Vince said, "and we're prepared to forgive you. Come with us, tonight, and you won't regret it. We promise you."

Robin stared at them in disbelief.

"Come with you—you mean you still expect me to—"

"Who else do you have, dear?" Amy asked. "Not that husband of yours."

"We heard about that—" Vince said, but Robin cut him off while still managing to keep her voice down.

"Heard about it?" she repeated. "My God, you did it, didn't you? You hurt Frank."

"I think you have that wrong, Robin," Amy said. "Frank has hurt you, and left you with no one—"

"That's what you think," Robin snapped. "That's what you planned, and *hoped,* but believe me that's not the case."

She watched Vince and Amy exchange a glance that could only be described as . . . hurt.

"You mean . . . you still won't come with us?" Vince asked.

"Not now," Robin said, coldly, "not ever."

They exchanged another glance and then Vince started to say, "More bad things can happen—"

"Don't threaten me!" Robin said, cutting him off. "Or you'll get another visit from Detective Jones." It was lame, but all she could come up with at the moment.

"Robin?"

The three of them turned at the sound of another voice. Brenda approached them, having apparently left the young artist elsewhere.

"Brenda," Robin said, with relief. She had an ally.

Brenda came up alongside Robin and faced the Wheatons.

"Why don't you introduce me to your friends?" Brenda asked.

"They're not my friends," Robin said. "I think you know who they are."

Vince and Amy were both smiling at Brenda ever so politely, but their smiles soon froze as Brenda lit into them with controlled fury.

"You're the two lowlifes who have been giving my friend a pretty hard time," Brenda said, with a smile. "Two sick individuals who should be off somewhere lying down with dogs instead of mingling with decent people." Robin had always wished that she could be as cool and calm as Brenda and still get her point across.

Vince and Amy glared at her, astonished.

"Let me tell you two something," Brenda continued. "You'll leave my friend alone from now on or you'll have me to deal with, and believe me when I say I don't play nice—not with creatures like you."

"Miss—" Vince started, but Brenda did not allow him to get any further than that.

"Don't 'Miss' me," Brenda said. "The two of you turn around and walk out before I start telling all these nice people what lowlife trailer trash you really are."

"Bren—" Robin started, trying to keep her friend from starting a scene.

"It's all right, Robin," Amy said, recovering her composure well before her spouse. "Your friend seems very protective of you. I guess you never told us how protective. Brenda, isn't it?"

"That's right," Brenda said, "Brenda Telford. Remember the name."

"Oh," Amy said, sweetly, "we will, don't worry. Sweetheart?" she said to Vince. "I think we've overstayed our welcome."

She turned him and walked him towards the door, with Robin and Brenda watching them until they were outside.

"The goddamned nerve!" Brenda said.

"You were . . . spectacular," Robin said.

"I was, wasn't I?" Brenda asked. "I saw them from across the room and knew who they were immediately. My God, you were right. They're both beautiful. She has the perfect little body to actually wear a jumpsuit like that! Tacky as it was! And him. What a hunk."

"Just be careful of Miss Perfect and Mr. Hunk, Brenda," Robin said. "I'm not sure they've ever been spoken to that way before."

"Well," Brenda said. "They just better stop messing with my friend." Brenda put an arm around Robin protectively.

"We better get back to the party," Robin said.

"That's what I came to tell you," Brenda said. "I'm leaving."

"With who?"

"That adorable little artist," Brenda said. "He wants to take my picture."

"He's a little young—"

"He's twenty-five, my dear," Brenda said, "and very talented . . . and, I think, horny." She giggled and added, "But I intend to find out for sure."

"He's going to leave his own showing?"

"What can I say?" she asked. "He wants to shoot me."

"Brenda," Robin said, "be careful . . ."

"I can handle him, Robin," Brenda said. "He's a pussycat."

"No," Robin said, "I mean be real careful. There's a possibility that Vince and Amy may have had something to do with what happened to Frank."

"Well," Brenda said, "if either of your beautiful

friends—ex-friends—tries to come near me they're going to find me a lot harder to deal with than Frank. I mean, no offense, Robin, but he is a writer and writers are not exactly the physical type."

"Bren, I'm serious—"

"So am I," Brenda said, spotting the artist across the floor, smiling at her. "Isn't he cute? All that long, beautiful hair? I'll call you tomorrow and let you know everything that happens."

Brenda leaned in, kissed Robin's cheek and was off so quickly that she didn't have a chance to respond. Robin watched her friend leave arm-in-arm with the artist and was glad, at least, that Brenda was leaving with a man, and not alone.

"Robin?"

She turned to see Caroline standing there.

"Your friend has left?" Caroline asked. "What a shame."

The look on her face and the tone of her voice convinced Robin that Brenda was right. Caroline was a bitch.

TWENTY-SIX

Carlos Beltre stared down at the naked woman as she slept in his bed. They had made love as soon as they got into his apartment. She was older than he by several years, probably five or six. She told him she was twenty-eight, but he suspected thirty. When they'd met his photographer's eye had immediately identified her as a perfect subject. He knew she was wearing a push up bra, but he also knew that when she was naked her breasts would be perfect, albeit small.

She was an energetic and eager lover and they had romped in his bed for hours before she finally drifted off to sleep. When her breathing became even and regular he had risen from the bed and gone to his studio for his Nikon. He would start shooting her while she slept and then awaken her for more photos.

He shot her in black and white first, starting when she was on her back, small, hard breasts flattening only slightly, blonde hair bushy between her legs, creeping up her belly. The amount of pubic hair she flaunted had excited him. Most women his age shaved down there, preferring to show less hair, artfully shaped, rather than the wild, tangled bush this woman had.

She moved while she slept, rolling onto her side. He shot the line of her back and the curve of her buttocks. He was about to move to the other side of the bed when the knock came at the door. Had he been asleep he might not have heard it. She didn't hear it, and slept on.

He left the bedroom and entered the studio, flicking on

the special lights he'd had installed which illuminated the room like daylight. He walked to the door, camera in hand. As he reached the door the knock came again, gentle but insistent. He couldn't imagine who it was, but it would serve them right for knocking so late if they were shocked by his nudity. He was very happy with his own body, which had only eight percent body fat, and often walked around his apartment naked. More than one mail man—or woman—had gasped when he opened the door. This couldn't be mail, though, or UPS, as it was too late.

"This better be good—" he started as he opened the door but he caught his breath when he saw the beautiful woman standing there, naked. She was small and perfectly proportioned.

"Take my picture?" she cooed, cocking a hip and posing.

As he opened his mouth to speak the man stepped into view, also naked, his muscles rippling as he moved. Carlos couldn't help but notice the man was huge all over.

"What the—"

That was when the man struck him with the palm of his hand in the chest. The blow would leave no mark, but it caused the man to stagger back, stunned and momentarily out of breath. He dropped his Nikon, which clicked off one picture when it struck the floor.

The naked couple entered quickly. The man straddled Carlos, who could now only see that huge penis hovering above him. Was this a rape, he wondered? Were they going to rape him?

This was his last thought as the man struck him again, knocking him unconscious.

TWENTY-SEVEN

Jones came into the office the next day and, as had become his habit, checked on the cases that had come in during the night. He knew none of them would be assigned to him, but he checked each day out of curiosity. That was when he saw the one murder that had come in . . .

He picked up the report and looked at it again, read the description of the victim. Then he checked to see who had responded to the scene. Thankfully, it hadn't been Detective Winston. Instead, it had been a detective named Singleton. There was little difference, really, except that Singleton was younger and less bitter. He still had no use for Jones, though. Even though he hadn't been around very long, he'd heard all the stories about Jones and his bad streak with partners.

He looked around and saw two of the day crew seated at their desks.

"Did Singleton go home?" he asked.

"Soon as his shift was over," Detective Carl Miller said.

Jones looked around again and his eyes fell on the closed door of his boss's office.

"Is he in?"

Miller looked up and saw Jones looking at the office door.

"Oh, he's in there," the other man said, "but he's in a foul mood."

Jones knew that would make his boss even harder to talk to, but he felt he had no choice. He went up to the door and knocked.

"Come!" came the voice from inside.

He opened the door and entered. Captain Joe Phillips sat behind his desk, glowering. His chair was back in a leaning position and he was rubbing his stomach.

"What is it, Jones?" Phillips demanded. "I'm busy."

"You've got a killing on your desk, boss, from last night," Jones said.

"The woman?"

"Right."

"What about it? It's Singleton's case, isn't it?"

"Yes, it is." Jones closed the door and approached the desk. "In his report he says there was no family to notify, and no one to identify the body. I mean, they found a wallet with a license, but they didn't get anyone to go to the morgue and make an actual I.D."

"So?"

"So I know who the woman is," Jones said. "I know who can I.D. the body."

"So tell Singleton."

Jones dropped the carbon of the case file on his superior's desk.

"I want you to assign this case to me."

"You're trying to steal the kid's case?" Phillips asked.

"No," Jones said, "I'm not, but it's connected to the case I'm working on."

Phillips frowned. His face was heavily lined and Jones often wondered if that was because he was in his late fifties, or if his face had always been that way.

"What are you working on?"

"The stalking of the woman who works at the Art Museum."

"I thought that wasn't even a stalking?" his superior asked. "That it had only been two days. Besides, you were only sent there to appease her."

"I started to think there might actually be something to it, and I think I was right."

"What's that got to do with this killing?"

"The victim is my victim's best friend."

"And?"

"Cap," Jones said, "I can notify Mrs. Lobianco—my victim—about her friend's death. She can I.D. the body, or lead us to some family."

"Give the info to Singleton."

"I think the cases are connected," Jones said, "and I also think the Forest Park thing is connected."

"Forest Park . . ." Phillips repeated, his frown depending. "Wait a minute, the guy in the park with the drugs. He's your victim's husband, right?"

"Right," Jones said. "Do you see the coincidence here? All three cases are linked."

"There's coincidence, all right," Phillips said, "but you think the perp is the same?"

"I do."

"But I thought they had a perp in this one," Phillips said. He scanned the top of his desk for the file, then reached over and grabbed the copy of the report Jones had brought in with him. "They found this photographer guy hanging from a pipe in his own apartment. Singleton figures he did the girl, then himself."

"I'd like to look into it, anyway."

Phillips made a face and hissed.

"Damned ulcer is going to eat me up from the inside out," he complained. "And you're not helping."

"Look, Cap," Jones said, "there's too much coincidence to allow Winston, Singleton and me to work on this thing separately. Partner me with Singleton and give us the three cases."

Phillips's frown deepened into a scowl and he said, "Sit down, Jack."

Jones sat and waited. He knew what was coming.

"You were a hell of a detective once, Jack," Phillips said, "until you started having your difficulties. Until your . . . lifestyle changed."

Jones tried to control his temper.

"If this is about my wife's profession—"

"Can it!" Phillips said. "I don't give a flying fuck what your wife does for a living. Getting married is a change of lifestyle. That's all I meant. You lost some partners, you got married, you lost your focus—"

"I'm focused on this, sir."

"Are you?"

"Yes, sir."

"If I give you these cases somebody is going to get pissed."

"If you don't, sir," Jones said, "I'll be pissed . . . with all due respect."

Phillips regarded him for a few seconds, then said, "I'm going to take your word for this, Jack. I don't have the patience to review all three files."

"You have all the pertinent facts on which to base a decision, sir," Jones said. "All the victims are connected."

"Except this guy," Phillips said, "the one who hung himself."

"Maybe."

Phillips tapped his desk with one hand and continued to rub his belly with the other. Then he poured himself some water from a carafe on his desk, grabbed an antacid out of his desk drawer and ate it.

"What the hell," he said. "If someone's going to get pissed it might as well be Winston. He's a pain in the ass anyway."

"Thank you, sir."

"I'll tell him and Singleton myself," Phillips said. "They won't like it any better coming from me, but they won't react as badly as if it came from you."

"Yes, sir," Jones said, standing.

"Jack," Phillips said, "clean this up for me and I'll put you back on the charts and start you catching normal cases again."

"Yes, sir."

"Fuck it up and you're out."

Jones didn't know if Phillips meant out of the squad or out of a job completely, and he didn't ask.

"Yes, sir," he said.

"Work the case today yourself," Phillips said. "You can team with Singleton starting tomorrow morning."

"Fine."

Jones started for the door and Phillips said, "Do us all a favor."

"What's that?" Jones asked from the door.

"Wrap it all up by tonight," Phillips said. "Maybe there'll be less people pissed that way."

"I'll give it my best shot, sir," he said, even though he thought his boss was being facetious.

At least, he hoped he was.

TWENTY-EIGHT

Jones had two choices. He could go to Robin's and give her the news, or he could stop by the apartment where it happened and take a look around. He decided to go to the crime scene first, before something happened to contaminate it. Maybe he'd still get to Robin before she read a newspaper. It was a chance he'd have to take to get a look at a clean crime scene.

The apartment was in a section of the city called Soulard. It was part residential and partially lined with clubs and restaurants. It was an artistic part of town, where artists and musicians liked to live.

When Jones arrived at the apartment he was surprised there wasn't a cop out front. This was an active investigation, after all. More than likely Singleton had accepted the homicide/suicide aspect of the case and had not posted a guard. He was, after all, a young detective and inexperienced.

The keys to the apartment had been taken in as evidence and placed in the property room, from where Jones had retrieved them. He let himself into the hall, then slit the crime scene tape that sealed the door after Forensics finished up and went inside.

He stopped just inside the door to look around. The lights were on in the place and it was very bright. He looked up and saw that track lighting with what appeared to be special bulbs had been installed. That wasn't surprising, since it was a photographer's studio.

The man had been found hanging from a pipe in the studio, a fallen chair beneath him. In the bedroom the woman had been found on the bed, slashed to death. Jones had gone into work early and there were no M.E. or Forensic reports yet—apparently, they hadn't been finished yet—but Singleton had observed that there were multiple wounds. Both the man and woman had been naked, and there were semen stains on the sheets. Singleton assumed a rendezvous, and then a fight. The blood and semen stained sheets had been removed, but both stains had soaked through to the mattress.

Jones went back into the studio and walked around. He was waiting for something to jump out at him, something that would tell him a story. He saw the shelves where the man had kept his cameras. He also found a stack of invitations to a showing, apparently the art show where the photographer had met and picked up Brenda. He assumed this because Brenda's evening clothes had also been taken in as evidence. If the man had a showing the night before, it made sense to assume that they had met there. He'd ask Robin. This kind of "art" show should certainly have attracted her.

The walls of the studio were covered with photos, obviously taken by Beltre. Many of them were nudes, some in color and some in black-and-white. Jones thought that the black-and-white ones looked much more erotic.

He stood beneath the pipe the man, Beltre, had been found hanging from and looked up. He tried to imagine standing on a chair, putting a rope around his own neck and then kicking the chair away. How far would the chair go? He looked around and there was a fallen chair several feet away, but he wouldn't know if that was where it had landed until he saw some of the crime scene photos.

After examining the photos on the wall he went back to the cameras on the shelves. He picked up a Minolta and looked at it. Examining the back it appeared to have no film in it. He opened it and confirmed this. He picked up three more cameras and found the same to be true, until he grabbed a Nikon. It had film, a roll that had only been partially shot. Did photographers keep their cameras empty when they weren't in use? And if so, did this mean that Beltre had been using this one? Jones turned it over in his hands and saw that a corner of the case was cracked. Had it been dropped? Or, perhaps, knocked from his hands? Would a man like Beltre, who photographed women in the nude, pass up the chance of shooting a woman he was sleeping with? Were there pictures of Brenda on this roll?

He examined the other cameras on the shelf, but the Nikon was the only one with film in it.

Jones spent several more minutes in the place, but when he left all he took away with him was that Nikon camera and one of the postcard type invitations. He'd take it down to the lab and have someone develop it after he spoke with Robin.

He and Katy had played Farmer's Daughter the night before and while that game usually took a lot out of him, he'd found himself oddly unable to sleep that morning. Getting started that early would enable him to get to Robin's apartment before she left for work.

Robin had a cup of coffee in her hand when she came to the door.

"Good morning," she said. "I can offer you coffee but that's about it, if I don't want to be—" She stopped short when she saw the look on his face. "What is it?"

"Robin, I have some bad news." He took hold of her shoulders.

"Is it Frank?" she asked. "Has something happened to Frank?"

"No," he said, "Frank's fine. It's . . . Brenda."

"Brenda?" Her eyes went wide and she covered her mouth with her hands. "What happened?"

"She's dead, Robin," he said. "Somebody killed her."

TWENTY-NINE

"What? Who?" Robin stammered with disbelief. "She left last night with a man, an artist—"

"A photographer named Beltre?"

"That's him."

"He's dead, too."

"My God!"

"Come on," he said, stepping inside and closing the door behind him, "let's sit down."

He led her to the sofa, where they sat side by side. He took her hands in his. They were like ice. Then she leaned forward suddenly and began to cry into his chest. What surprised him was that he didn't feel awkward at all. He held her until she finished, then leaned back and apologized to him.

"That's all right," he assured her. "I understand."

"What happened?" she asked. "How—how did she . . ."

"On the surface it looks as if they went back to his apartment and had sex," Jones explained, "then had a fight. He killed her, then hung himself."

"What?"

"That's how it looks."

She looked at him carefully.

"But you don't think it happened that way?"

"Were you at this art show last night?" He showed her the postcard invitation.

"Yes," she said, "that's where Brenda met Beltre. It was his show."

"And who else was there?"

Her eyes widened as if she just remembered.

"They were!"

"The Wheatons?"

"Yes," she said. "Oh, my God. Brenda . . . she told them off. They killed her!"

He tried to calm her.

"It's a possibility," he said. "Tell me what happened?"

"The Wheatons showed up and I couldn't believe it. I—I guess I forgot they were invited. I might have even sent them the invitation myself weeks ago, before this all started."

"Then what happened?"

"They came up to me and I—I told them to get away from me. I accused them of hurting Frank and they were just so . . . so calm. It was infuriating, but I couldn't make a scene there."

"And then?"

"And then Brenda came over and in a very calm, controlled voice called them vile names and basically told them that if they messed with me they'd have to mess with her."

"What happened then?"

"They left, and then Brenda left with Carlos."

"How soon after the Wheatons left did Brenda and Beltre leave?"

"I don't know . . . probably ten or fifteen minutes."

"They could have waited outside and followed them. They waited until Beltre and Brenda went to bed, gave them enough time to have sex . . . what did Brenda say she and Beltre were going to do?"

"She said she thought he was horny and was going to find out."

"Anything else?"

"Yes," Robin said, closing her eyes to bring it all back, "she said Carlos wanted to shoot her."

"Shoot her? You mean, take her picture?"

"Yes."

"I found one camera in the apartment with film in it. The whole roll wasn't shot. Do you know if a professional photographer would leave film in his camera when he's done with it?"

"I—I don't know that much about photographers," she said. "What are you thinking?"

"I'm thinking that maybe he was taking her picture and there was a knock on the door," Jones theorized. "He went to answer it. Maybe it was the Wheatons. Maybe not. Whoever it was killed both of them, and he never had a chance to finish the roll. The Wheatons—or whoever the killer was—picked up his camera and put it on the shelf with the others."

"Picked it up?"

"It's cracked," he said. "They must have hit him as soon as he opened the door. Okay, try this." He took a moment to form his thoughts. "Brenda is asleep. Beltre wakes up and decides to take her picture while she's asleep. That's when they come to the door. They probably knock, and she doesn't hear it. He does, goes to the door, and they attack him as soon as he opens the door. He drops the camera—is Brenda a sound sleeper?"

"Like a log," Robin said, "especially after sex."

"Okay, so she doesn't wake up—and maybe she never did."

"Was she—how was she killed?"

"Multiple stab wounds."

"Oh God . . ." She closed her eyes and the tears she'd been fighting squeezed out. "Is there any chance she didn't feel . . . feel anything . . ."

"Maybe," he said, "if the first wound was the killing wound. After they killed her they strung him up and made it look as if he killed himself. People would believe that, wouldn't they? Artistic people are volatile people, right? Hot-tempered? Maybe he'd kill her and then himself out of remorse?"

"It could be," she said. "I—I didn't know him that well."

"Who did?"

"Caroline . . . it was her gallery we were in last night."

"Would Caroline have been sleeping with him?"

"Probably," she said. "She likes young artists, and Carlos is—was—young."

"Robin, you have to help me."

"Do you—are you working on this case?"

"I'm working on all three," he said, "yours, Frank's and Brenda's. I got my boss to give me all of them."

"Thank God," she said. "You'll get Vince and Amy. I know you will."

"I'll need your help."

"What can I do?"

"Call your friend Caroline. Tell her what happened, ask her if this Beltre was the type to explode in rage, and then feel remorse. Can you do that?"

"Y-yes. What else?"

"Did you get a lawyer for Frank?"

"Yes."

"I'm going to try to get him released from the hospital today, and then arraigned. Bail him out as quickly as possible, and then I want you and him to stay together. You'll be safer that way."

"All right," she said. "Can you do that?"

"I'll have to call a judge . . . maybe I can. If not today I can get it done by tomorrow morning."

"And then what?"

"And then you two stay together while I go after the Wheatons. I found out where they're from and I'll do some checking."

"You said before that you could arrest them if you had probable cause."

"That's right."

"And that I'd have to testify to . . . to everything."

"That's right."

"Well, I'm ready," she said.

"I can't arrest them for Brenda, Robin," Jones said, "only for threatening you. They'd get out on bail. I'll have to wait until I can get them for murder."

"They did it," she said, coldly. "I know they did. I saw the way Amy looked at Brenda, and how calm she was in the face of Brenda's name-calling. They killed her, Jack, and they hurt Frank. I don't care now who knows what I did, I'll testify."

"Okay," he said, patting her hands, "okay, you can testify, after I arrest them for murder."

They both stood up and he led her to the door.

"Get your purse. I want you to go to work. I don't want you to be alone."

"I—I don't know if I can work—not after Brenda—"

"Just go there and sit in your office," he said. "Tell that security guard that you're in danger. He's sweet on you."

She smiled.

"He thinks of me as a daughter—"

"Whatever," Jones said, doubting that. "Just go there and wait until you hear from me."

"What are you going to do?"

"I'm going to have to try to put together a case," he said,

"but I'll start by talking to Frank and getting him out."

"Will you tell him—"

"I'll only tell him what I need to, Robin," he said. "The rest is up to you. Come on, get your purse. I'll walk you to your car."

On the way to the car Robin asked, "Did Katy tell you about our lunch?"

He hesitated, then said, "Some of it."

"She didn't like me very much."

"Oh, I don't know—"

"I do," Robin said. "I can't blame her. I'm taking up a lot of your time."

"It's my job."

She put her hand on his arm. "No it isn't, not all of it. You've been very kind to me and I appreciate it."

Flustered, he said, "It's, ah, nothing."

"She's very beautiful—Katy, I mean."

"Yes, she is," Jones said, "and young—"

"I'm not judging," she said, as they reached her car. "Who am I to judge, after what I've done?"

"Robin, you've got to stop beating yourself up—"

"I may have caused all of this," she said, with her head down. "Frank, Bren—"

"We won't know that for a while."

She looked at him, then said, "I better get to work."

She got in her car and he closed the door. Katy had been right about one thing. This girl needed a lot of help.

THIRTY

Jones had a big day ahead of him. He could have used a partner, so he decided to go back to the office to call Singleton at home.

"Did the boss call you?" he asked when the young detective answered the phone.

"He did."

"And?"

"I'll do what the boss tells me to do, Jack."

"Well, I'm senior man, Singleton," Jones said, "and I could use your help today."

"Today's my day off."

"Put in for overtime," Jones said.

There was silence at the other end of the line.

"Come on, Singleton," Jones said. "I promise I won't get you killed today."

"I'm not worried about that," Singleton said.

"Yeah, right. Coming in?"

"Why don't you just tell me what you want me to do," Singleton said, "and I'll start from here?"

"Fine."

"And it's Ted."

"What?"

"My name's Ted."

"Okay, Ted," Jones said, "here's what we have to do. You tell me which part you want to take care of . . ."

It took Jones two hours to find a judge with whom he

could work to get Frank Lobianco freed right from the hospital, without spending a moment in a cell. It was a definite "for old times sake" kind of thing, as the judge remembered the same thing that Captain Phillips remembered—that Jack Jones was, at one time, a hell of a detective on the fast track to success. This enabled Jones to get Frank out that evening, instead of early the next morning.

Jones waited for Frank in the lobby of the hospital and conducted the man to his car.

"I'll drop you at the museum," he told Frank, "and then you and Robin find a hole and pull it in after you."

"I want to help," Frank said, "not hide."

"The only way you could help would be to identify Vince and Amy Wheaton as the people who attacked you."

"I can't do that," Frank said. "I was hit from behind."

"Then the only other way you can help," Jones said, "is to do what I tell you."

"And what are you going to do?"

"I'm going to find someone who can identify them."

THIRTY-ONE

When the door to Robin's office opened she looked up quickly.

"Oh, God, Robin," Frank said, holding his hands out in a placating gesture, "I didn't mean to scare you."

"Frank!" She'd been thinking about him for the past half-hour, and seeing him in the doorway made her stomach jump. She leaped up and ran into his arms.

"Hey, whoa!" Frank said. "Injured man, here."

But he didn't back away from the contact and he hugged her back just as hard.

In the face of everything that had happened all of her problems with Frank Lobianco seemed silly, now. She had been sitting at her desk all morning, going over the reasons she had asked for their separation, and none of them seemed so bad, anymore. The things she had done since their separation made her a terrible person, not him.

"Frank," she said, into his shoulder, "I'm so sorry for everything." Then she pulled her face away. "You smell like the hospital, and dirt."

He laughed and said, "All I had were the same clothes I was wearing the night I was attacked. I've got to go home and take a shower, and get some fresh clothes."

"Let's go, then," she said, turning and going to her desk for her purse. "Jack—Detective Jones said he wants us to stay together until we hear from him."

"That suits me," Frank said. "I've been trying to get

close to you for months."

She took his arm and said, "We'll talk about that."

Jones returned to the Major Case Squad office and found Ted Singleton there, sitting at Jones' desk and not his own.

"How'd you do?" Jones asked.

"Here are the pictures," Singleton said, tossing an envelope containing the photos from the dead man's camera onto Jones' side of the desk. "There's nothing there that I can see."

"What else?"

"You sent a request to the Omaha Police?"

"Right, after I ran a check on some plates." He'd almost forgotten. He'd found out that the Wheatons had an Omaha plate on their car. When he ran it the ownership came up to a Carl Brookens.

"I got an answer from the police there," Singleton said. "They've got nothing on a Carl Brookens, nothing on Vincent and Amy Wheaton."

"Great."

"What they do have," Singleton went on, "is an unsolved homicide."

"Who was killed?"

"A woman's boyfriend," Singleton said. "The facts are kind of odd."

"What are they?"

"Apparently," the young detective said, "the couple was fighting for a while, and the woman met some friends. She formed a relationship with these friends, which went bad. After that she reported to the police that she was being stalked."

"By who?'

"Get this," Singleton said, "by a man and a woman—okay, here's your Brookens. The couple was Carl and Amanda Brookens. Apparently, they wanted the relationship with her to become sexual in nature and she wanted to call it off. From that point on she claimed they were stalking her." Singleton had been eyeing the computer printout he'd received from Omaha, and now looked up at Jones. "At some point the boyfriend was killed."

"Where and how?"

"In his apartment," Singleton said. "The police found drugs—not a lot, but enough to make them think he was selling. They assumed that was why he was killed."

"Did they question the Brookens couple?"

"Nope," Singleton said. "Couldn't find them. The case is still on their books as an open case."

They probably would not have put out an alarm on the Brookens couple. Not for stalking, and there wasn't enough evidence for them to put out warrants on them for suspicion of homicide. Same as the situation now with the Wheatons. Jones didn't have enough to get a warrant for them on the photographer double homicide. If he pulled them in for questioning they'd probably do another disappearing act. They were a slick couple, whatever name they used.

"If he was killed for drugs," Jones asked, "why were there drugs still in the apartment?"

Singleton thought a moment, then said, "Good question. I've got one for you, though. Have you ever heard of a couple stalking someone? That's a new one on me."

"Ted," Jones said, "maybe I better bring you up to speed on this case."

After leaning back and clasping his hands behind his neck, listening to Jones' recap, Singleton lowered his hands and sat forward. He rubbed at his nose with his right index finger before speaking. Jones knew he was taking just a little bit more time before forming his thoughts into words.

"Okay," he said.

"Okay? What do you mean, okay?"

"I mean, okay, I can see why you wanted these three cases," Singleton said, "but how do you think Winston is going to react to this?"

"He'll piss and moan," Jones said. "Let the boss handle him."

"Okay then," Singleton said, "we don't have any proof that your couple—the Wheatons—are the same stalking couple as the one in Omaha, but it sure would be a weird coincidence to have *two* stalking couples."

"Yes, it would."

"And we don't have any proof that they killed the boyfriend in Omaha."

"No, we don't," Jones said, "but it can't just be a coincidence that they attacked Robin's husband, Frank, and tried to frame him."

"Why not just kill him in his apartment, too?"

"I'm going to guess that they learned from what happened in Omaha," Jones proposed. "Maybe they didn't plan on killing the boyfriend. Maybe things just got out of hand."

"So here in St. Louis," Singleton said, "they decide to try and avoid killing."

"Right," Jones said, "but then later Brenda gets in their face and they end up killing her, and the artist. Things got out of hand again."

"Trying to frame the artist and make it look like a murder/suicide."

"Right."

"And we can't prove any of it. If we move too soon," the younger detective said, echoing Jones' thoughts, "we'll lose them."

"Right, again."

"So how do we get them?"

"Well, now," Jones said, "that's where you come in."

"Me? What do you mean?"

"You have a nice, fresh outlook on the situation," Jones said. "Suppose you tell me what you'd do next."

"Well, I'd—"

"I mean," Jones added, cutting the younger man off, "after you get out of my chair."

As Robin and Frank pulled away from the museum in Robin's car neither of them noticed the car that pulled out of the lot behind them. It followed them up Fine Arts Drive and out of the park at Hampton Avenue. And onto Highway 40.

"This is not the way she goes home," Vince said, as he drove their Chrysler behind Robin's Toyota.

"They must be going to his place," Amy said.

"I can't believe it," Vince said. "What is she doing with him?"

"Obviously," Amy answered, "Robin is much more loyal than we thought."

"You'd think she would have learned something from the death of her friend."

"If she even knows about it yet," Amy said. "Maybe we should call her and tell her."

"What about that detective?"

"I don't think we have to worry about him," Amy said. "Once she knows about what happened to her friend she'll make her decision."

"I hope she makes the right one," he said. "For her sake."

"Whatever decision she makes," Amy said, "I'm afraid we're finished here in St. Louis. We can't stay much longer after . . ." She left it unsaid that things had again gotten out of control.

"Good," Vince said, "I was getting bored with her, anyway. And if she's not with us, I couldn't bear to stay."

"I feel the same way, my sweet," Amy said, stroking his face.

THIRTY-TWO

Jones looked through the photographs as he listened to Singleton's suggestions for a course of action. Obviously, the photographer had decided to take pictures of the sleeping, naked Brenda after they'd had sex. He had to admit that Robin's friend had a very nice body, long and lean, almost like his wife Katy except without the implants. The man had apparently been able to click away without waking her, although she had seemed to move around a bit in her sleep.

In addition to noticing the subject of the photos, however, he also noticed that the man seemed very good at what he did. These photos were as good or better than some of the stuff on his wall. The shots of Brenda were kind of dark, but Jones had the feeling that the artist was just getting the feel of his subject and was shooting in the dark, not wanting to chance waking Brenda with a flash of light. As a pro, he probably had a camera that shot pictures in low light.

Then he came to the last picture, which was different in subject and conformity. For one thing, it was much brighter, and had obviously not been shot in the same room. Also, it had been shot at an odd angle. He had to turn the photo on one of the corners in order to right it and what he saw excited him.

A woman's butt.

"Are you listening?" Singleton asked.

"Did you look at these?"

"Yeah," the young detective said. "Girl had a killer

body, but I kinda like more tits on my women. Although I do kinda wish my wife had an ass that sweet."

"Which ass?" Jones asked.

"What do you mean? The girl on the bed. The dead girl."

"What about this one?" He showed Singleton the last photo.

"Same girl, different shot," Singleton said. "Must have shot that one before they went into the bedroom."

"No," Jones said, taking the negatives out. "Look here, you can see that this was the last picture taken."

"Okay," Singleton said, "so it was last."

"But the girl in this picture is standing up."

"So?" Singleton said, again. "She woke up while he was shooting her, and started to pose."

"But she was killed in bed."

Singleton sighed aloud and said, "The killer took her back to bed and did her."

"Ted," Jones said, "take a good look at this picture, and this picture." He handed the young detective a picture of the dead girl's butt, and then the butt in the last photo.

Singleton studied them and then said, "It could be the same—"

"No," Jones said. He got up and stood next to Singleton. He pointed. "This is the girl on the bed. This is a nice clear shot of her butt. Right?"

"Right."

"Now look at the other one. Different butt."

"It's hard to tell," Singleton said. "There's so much light in this last photo and so little light on the other one."

"Okay," Jones said, "forget that for now. Look at the angle of the shot."

"Artsy," Singleton said, with a shrug.

"Accidental," Jones said.

"What do you mean?"

"I mean the camera these pictures were taken with had a crack in it," Jones said. "I think he dropped it when he was attacked, and it clicked off this last picture."

"Of the girl's butt."

"Of his killer's butt."

"What?"

"What's that?" Jones asked, pointing to the brighter photo.

Singleton peered at the photo and asked, "Where?"

"Right at the base of her spine, where her butt cleavage is. See it?"

"A smudge?"

"No," Jones said, taking the photo back. "Not a smudge. She's got something on her ass, something the other girl doesn't have. And look here, just to the outside. Is that someone else's leg?"

"You're saying that the photographer accidentally took a picture of not one killer, but two? And they're naked?"

"Maybe."

"Why would they be naked?"

Jones sat back down at his desk and started to rummage through his desk.

"Because they were going to get splattered with blood," Jones said. "Did the lab boys go over the whole apartment?"

"Yea, they did."

"Check the file," Jones said. "See what they found in the bathroom. Also, see what they said about bloody handprints or footprints."

He continued to search his desk drawers while Singleton read the file.

"Here it is," he said. "They took some hairs out of the shower drain—the victim's hair, and some other hair, as well."

"From how many people?"

"Two or three."

"Any match the female victim?"

"No," Singleton said, and then his eyes brightened.

"What about prints in blood?"

"There were some, but they were wiped. They got towels with blood and they typed it. Two different types." He looked at Jones incredulously. "The killers took a shower after they killed these two people?"

"That's one way to get the blood off," Jones said. "As for the hair we don't know how many women this guy's had in his shower but—damn it!" He slammed his drawer.

"What are you looking for?"

"I was sure I had a magnifying glass," Jones said. "I want to get a clearer look at this picture. There are two things here that can help us, and I can't make them out. We'll have to have the lab blow it up."

"That'll take time," Singleton said. "I have a better idea."

"What?"

"I'll show you, Jack," he said, taking the photo from Jones. "Follow me."

"Where are we going?" Jones asked, hurrying after the younger man as he went out the door.

"I'm going to show you a miracle of modern technology," Singleton said.

THIRTY-THREE

When Robin walked into the apartment that she had shared with Frank for several years, she was surprised that she felt at home. She had not been back since the separation, but certainly would not have predicted this feeling of coming home.

"How does it feel to be back?" Frank asked.

"Good," she said. "It feels good."

"I have to shower," he said, "get the hospital smell off me."

"Are you hungry?" she asked.

"Starved."

"Is there any food in the kitchen?"

"I think you might find something," he said, "if it all hasn't spoiled while I was . . . away."

"I'll see what I can whip up for us," she said.

"I won't be long."

He came to her and took her hands. The gesture, and the look on his face, melted her heart.

"I'm glad you're here, Robin," he said, "whatever the circumstance."

She squeezed his hands and smiled, unable to find her voice at that moment.

Across the way from the apartment Vince and Amy sat in their car.

"What do we do now?" he asked.

"We wait, my sweet," she said. "Like we did with her friend and the photographer."

Vince remembered what they had done to Robin's friend and her lover and immediately he was erect. Amy noticed. She reached over and laid her hand over her husband's crotch.

"Patience, my love," she said. "Tonight we'll get our final answer from her."

"And if she doesn't come with us?"

She squeezed him through his pants and said, "She'll have to pay the price."

Suddenly, Vince wasn't all that sure which way he wanted Robin's decision to take them.

Robin found tuna fish, cream of mushroom soup and a can of peas in the almost bare cupboard and managed a tuna casserole by the time Frank came out, wearing a robe she had bought for him several Christmases ago.

"Smells good," he said, sniffing the air. "This place lost your smell about a month after you left, and I haven't been able to get it back."

"Sit down at the table," she said. "It's almost ready."

She had set the table with place mats, glasses of ice water and silverware. Frank had been eating out of cans and cartons, sometimes over the sink, since she left.

As he sat she came in with the casserole, set it down on the table so they could help themselves, and then sat across from him in what was for years her customary place. She looked around at the familiar surroundings and felt a pang of regret at having left. What had she been thinking? So they had some problems. What couples didn't? Look what had happened to them because she had chosen to run away from them instead of trying to solve them together.

She knew Frank wanted her back, but would he want her when she told him what she had done?

"What are you thinking?" he asked, spooning tuna onto their plates.

"We have to talk, Frank," she said.

"We've had to talk for a long time, Robin," he said. "Neither of us has been very good at it."

She smiled and said, "You're sweet to want to take some of the blame, but we're in this mess because of decisions I've made—and some of those decisions have been . . . well . . ."

"Let's talk after we eat, all right?" he said. "I'm really hungry, and I'd like to enjoy you being here with me before we start talking about things that might . . . change the mood. Can we do that?"

"Sure, Frank," she said, picking up her fork. "We can do that."

Actually, it was a reprieve for her and one she appreciated—but right after they finished eating they were going to talk, as they had never talked before.

Detective Jack Jones watched as his new partner, Detective Ted Singleton, "scanned" the photo into a computer. Jones knew the bare minimum about computers, but Singleton seemed well versed and knew what he was doing.

"Tell me what this is going to do again?"

Singleton straightened and faced Jones while the computer whirred and clicked.

"I'm scanning the photo into the computer so we can put it on the monitor. Once I've done that we can make it clearer, or zoom in, or do whatever we want without having to wait for someone else to blow it up for us."

"I'll be damned," Jones said.

Singleton sat down in front of the computer. They waited for the scanner noises to stop, and then he started off a new cacophony by hitting some of the keys. And then, as if by magic, there was the photo on the screen.

"Okay," Singleton said, "I get into the right program, and . . . what do you want to do?"

"Well," Jones said, "why don't we get right to it? Show me what that is on her butt."

"Right."

As Jones watched, Singleton isolated the area they wanted, right above the gorgeous butt cleavage of the woman in the photo.

"Now I have to clear it up . . ." Singleton said, using the mouse rather than the keyboard, and what was once a smudge became very, very clear.

"Is that what I think it is?" Jones asked.

Singleton touched the screen and said, "It sure is, Jack. It's a tattoo of a rose."

THIRTY-FOUR

Robin finished cleaning up after the impromptu dinner and joined Frank on the living room sofa. She thought it odd that she hadn't sat on that sofa in several months, but there they were, in their customary positions and it felt so normal—almost.

"Want to watch *Change of Heart*?" he asked, picking up the TV remote.

"Frank," she said, taking the remote from his hand, "I told you I had something to talk to you about."

"Yes, you did," Frank said, giving her his full attention. He reached out and touched her arm, rubbing it. "I'm so glad you're here."

"Frank . . . this is so hard."

"Come on, Robin," he said. "You can tell me anything." He moved closer to her.

She'd forgotten how nice he looked after a shower, when his hair was all clean and "poofy." Frank Lobianco was certainly no hunk, like Vince Wheaton, but then he wasn't a crazy man, either. He was thoughtful and sweet and willing to do anything for her. That certainly made him her type. She loved his face, and his hands and she wondered again what she had been thinking all these months.

As if reading her mind Frank moved even closer, then leaned in and kissed her. She closed her eyes and surrendered to the touch of his lips on hers. He tasted of tuna, and slightly of toothpaste, and mostly of Frank.

"Frank," she said, pulling away, "I have to tell you—"

"You don't have to tell me anything, Robin," he said, putting his finger to her lips. "I don't care what happened while we were separated. I only care that we're together, here, now. I don't really know what's going on, and I don't know if you're going to come back to me. I just know that you're here, and I love you."

She leaned forward to press her forehead to his and said, "I love you, too, Frank."

He held her tightly while she sobbed into his shoulder, and then a little bit later he stood up, taking her with him. He clicked off the lamp and walked them both into the bedroom . . .

"No lights," Vince said, craning his neck to look up at the building. They'd already identified the second-floor windows of the apartment where Robin had lived with Frank before separating.

"We'll give them a little more time," Amy said.

"Shall we go in the same way as last time?" her husband asked.

"Definitely," Amy said. She always knew not wearing underwear would come in handy some day.

Now that they'd identified the tattoo on the butt of the woman in the picture, Singleton switched his focus to another part of the photo.

"That's a leg, all right," he said, pointing to the monitor, "a man's leg." He looked up at Jones, who was standing behind him. "Looks like our stalking couple has become a killing couple."

"Looks like it," Jones said, "but we can't prove it, yet."

"All we have to do is have them come in and show us her ass," Singleton said.

"You don't just haul a woman in and look at her butt, Ted," Jones said.

"Then we need someone who's already seen her butt who can identify the tattoo."

"Right."

"What about Mrs. Lobianco?"

"A definite possibility," Jones said. "Also the woman in Omaha."

"Split 'em up?" Singleton asked.

"I'll take Robin Lobianco," Jones said, "you take Omaha. Is her phone number in the file?"

"I think so," Singleton said, "if not I'll call the local police again."

Jones looked around, spotted an empty desk with a phone. Singleton could use the one next to the computer.

"Let's do it," he said.

Out in the parking lot Amy Wheaton put her hand on her husband's knee and said, "It's time. Let's go."

They got out of the car together, closing the doors as quietly as they could. They crossed to the door of Frank and Robin's condo building and entered, lucky that one of the tenants had left it unlocked. Vince and Amy considered themselves lucky, though, in general. They thought they led charmed lives, and that things would always go their way. And if they did not—well, they could always make an adjustment so that they would, once again.

Attacking Robin's husband and trying to frame him, that had been an adjustment. Killing Robin's friend Brenda, that had also been an adjustment. And what they would end up doing in the next half hour—well, that would probably be the biggest adjustment, of all.

* * * * *

Jones hung up and looked at Singleton, who was talking on his phone rather animatedly. Robin and Frank had not answered. Either they weren't there, or they'd decided not to answer the phone in case it was the Wheatons calling. He should have set up some kind of signal with them, to ring twice, hang up, and ring again, or something. It was his fault for not thinking ahead.

Singleton turned in his chair to look at him and held up one finger, telling him to be patient.

Once they had an eyewitness to the fact that Amy Wheaton had a tattoo of a rose on her butt they'd be able to go and pick up the couple for questioning. And if the woman in Omaha didn't know, or didn't want to say, or actually said that Amy *didn't* have such a tattoo, there was still the possibility that she had gotten it here in St. Louis. If that was the case then it was Robin who would have to verify it.

Singleton hung up, stood up and came over to the desk Jones was sitting at.

"Well?" the older detective asked.

"Her phone number was in the file. It took a lot of talking to finally get her to admit that yes, she did have sex with both Vince and Amy Wheaton."

"And?"

Singleton looked unhappy. "She never saw a tattoo on Amy Wheaton's butt."

"That leaves Robin," Jones said.

"What did she say?"

Jones stood up. "There was no answer. They may just not be answering the phone."

"What do you want to do?"

"Let's get over there and find out," Jones said. Both men left the room and hurried down the hall to their own office to retrieve their jackets. "If she verifies the existence of a tattoo—"

"What if she won't do it in front of her husband?"

Jones paused in the act of donning his jacket and said, "I think the time may have come for Robin to make a decision."

THIRTY-FIVE

Jones had a quick change of mind when he and Singleton got to the street and headed for their cars.

"Ted, you go over to Robin Lobianco's and see if that's where they are," he said. "I'll go to Frank Lobianco's place to see if they're just not answering the phone." All he had told them was to stay together. Now he wished he'd told them where.

"What about backup?" Singleton asked.

"Call for some when you get there if you think you need it," Jones said. "If there's going to be trouble, though, it's more likely I'll run into it than you."

"Then maybe I should be going with you, instead of—" the younger detective argued.

"Ted," Jones said, covering his exasperation, "I just want to cover all the bases, okay? Go to Robin's and if there's a problem I'll get to you on the radio."

"Well, okay," Singleton finally agreed, reluctantly, "what's the address?"

Frank rolled off of Robin and lay next to her.

"Wow!" he said.

"Maybe we should separate more often," she said, putting one hand over her heart, which was still pounding.

He turned his head and looked at her.

"It was never like that before, was it?" The question was rhetorical. They both knew that the sex had never been like that before.

She rolled over and kissed his shoulder.

"I love you, Frank, and I'm so sorry—"

"I told you before," he said, cutting her off. "I don't care what happened while we were apart."

"Frank," she said, "we still have to talk . . . I mean, this was wonderful, but it doesn't fix everything."

"I know that, Robin," he said, "but this is a start. Hey, I've got some white wine in the fridge. How about a toast to a new start?"

"Frank—"

"I'll get it," he said, springing off the bed and grabbing his robe. That, in itself, was something new. In the past after sex he'd always roll over and go to sleep. Maybe this was a new start for them but she knew they could not do that until she came clean with him. He had to know everything before he made any decisions.

She stretched, feeling drowsy, and was dimly aware of the front doorbell ringing. It took a few seconds to sink in and then she heard Frank yell, "I'll get it!"

Now it was her turn to spring off the bed. Frank still didn't grasp the degree of danger that existed, and he might—

"Frank, don't open the door!"

Out in the hall Vince and Amy had disrobed. Naked, they did not even bother to look around. It was late, and their plans always worked out. If anyone came walking out of their condo now they'd get a shock, but it wouldn't interfere with what Vince and Amy were doing. There was a cabinet by the condo door with double doors beneath it. Vince put his knife down on it, opened it, found it empty and pushed their clothes into it, then closed the doors. Then he picked up the knife from the top of the cabinet. It was the same knife he had used on Brenda Telford. He'd taken it from the artist's kitchen, and he'd liked it so much he'd taken it with him when they left. He looked at Amy, marveling as he always did at how exquisitely beautiful she was. Amy nodded, and he rang the bell.

Frank was in the act of opening the door as Robin shouted out to him. One habit he'd never been able to break was not using the peephole. He turned to look down the hall at her as the door burst open, smacking him in the back of the head and knocking him off balance. He windmilled, his robe flapping open, and then fell to the floor.

Robin came running down the hall, heedless of the fact that she was naked, shouting, "Frank!"

She knelt by her fallen husband and looked up at the two people who stepped through the doorway. That they were naked registered with her second. The first thing that registered was who they were.

THIRTY-SIX

The third thing she noticed was the knife in Vince's hand.

"Is that the same knife you killed Brenda with?" she asked, surprised at how calm her voice was.

"Look, sweetie," Vince said, ignoring the question, "she's all ready for us."

Amy was already looking at Robin and Robin felt more naked than she'd ever felt before.

"What the hell—" Frank said, holding his hand to the back of his head.

"Frank, I'm sure you remember Vince and Amy Wheaton, the people who attacked you, and who killed Brenda."

Frank looked up at them, his eyes widening. "They're naked." And then he noticed that Robin was, too. "Here," he told her, starting to shrug out of his robe, "take this—"

"Don't worry, Frank," Amy said. "It's not the first time we've seen your wife naked."

"W-what?"

Robin closed her eyes. Why couldn't they have just killed them without getting into this?

"Frank—"

"You mean she didn't tell you?" Amy asked.

"Tell me what?"

"That my beautiful husband and I shared her one night?" Amy went on.

"Shared—" He looked at Robin. "What are they talking about?"

"Frank . . . I don't think now's the time—"

"Now's a great time," Vince said.

"Look at my husband, Frank," Amy said. She reached over and took Vince's heavy penis in her hand. "He's getting hard already, thinking about having Robin again."

"Again?" Frank looked at Robin. "Again?"

Robin touched his shoulder and said, "I've been trying to tell you . . ."

"That's what you've been trying to tell me tonight?" he demanded. "That you slept with . . . him?"

"Both of us," Amy said, with a smile. "It was glorious."

"And now we've come to take her with us," Vince said. He had the knife in his left hand and he was fondling his erection with his right.

Frank's head swiveled around again, causing it to throb even more. He fixed his eyes on Vince's face, instead of the man's huge penis or the woman's perfect breasts.

"Take her . . . where?"

"Away," Amy said. "Robin's coming with us."

"She wants to be with us," Vince said.

"I do not!" Robin snapped. "I told you both to leave me alone."

"You see, Frank," Amy said, "we have made Robin an offer and we're waiting for her final decision."

"I *gave* you my final decision the same day you asked me," Robin said. "No!"

"No?" Vince looked confused.

"You're not changing your mind?" Amy asked. "After all we've done for you?"

"What have you done for me?" Robin demanded.

"We've removed some of the negative influences from your life," Vince said.

"You killed my friend!" Robin said, her eyes flashing. If

she'd had a knife in *her* hand at that moment she thought she would happily kill both of *them.* "You hurt my husband."

"But he's still a negative influence on you," Vince said.

Amy added, "We're going to take care of that tonight."

"What are these people talking about?" Frank demanded to anyone who would answer. "And, for Chrissake, why are you naked?" This time he directed the question to them. "Can we all get dressed?"

"No," Vince said, "you're not going to need clothes, Frank."

"And blood is too hard to clean off our clothes," Amy said.

"Frank," Robin said, as the fear suddenly set in.

"What?"

"We're going to kill you, Frank," Amy said. "No hard feelings, but once you're gone we think Robin will make the right decision."

"What right decision?" Frank asked. "To go with you?"

"Of course," Vince said.

"You people are crazy!"

"Yes," Robin said, "they are, Frank."

Vince looked sad suddenly and said, "Amy, I think Robin's making the wrong decision."

"Yes, darling," Amy said. "We came here to give you a choice, Robin . . . and now you're not leaving us with one."

THIRTY-SEVEN

Jones parked his car and looked around the lot. He did not see the Lexus owned by the Wheatons. Neither did he recognize the Chrysler they had driven there in. He knew the number of Frank Lobianco's condo, but did not know which window it was.

He crossed to the front door, found it unlocked and entered. The building had two floors and there seemed to be only four units per floor. It was very much like the one Robin lived in, now. He wondered if that had been deliberate on her part.

As he started up the stairs his radio suddenly sprang into life, first with static and then with Ted Singleton's barely recognizable voice.

"Jack?"

"I hear you, Ted."

"Nothing here," Singleton said, shortly. They weren't really supposed to be speaking so informally on this frequency. "Nobody's home."

"Okay," Jones said, "you might as well go back to the office. I'll check here and get back to you."

"I can come there—"

"No," Jones said. "Go back to the office."

He didn't want Singleton there. If Vince and Amy were there it would be Singleton's luck to be the fourth partner Jones lost recently. Jones didn't think he could handle that.

He clipped the radio back to his belt, on the opposite hip from his gun. The weight of the gun was always comforting, but the weight of the radio was a nuisance, and he never carried one unless he had to.

This time he felt he had to, and it almost cost him his life.

"Get up, both of you," Vince said to Frank and Robin, "but slowly . . ."

Frank kept his eyes on Vince. The man was armed with a knife, it was true, but Frank felt he had to do something to get Robin to safety. After all, he told himself, at least Vince didn't have a gun.

Frank and Robin were slowly getting to their feet when they all suddenly heard sounds from the hall—static, a tinny voice—of a man coming through on a radio.

They looked at each other immediately, as did Vince and Amy. However, one couple was simply trying to give each other hope while the other had the man looking to the woman for guidance.

Next thing they knew the doorbell rang.

Amy waved her arm at Vince, who moved faster than Frank thought possible. The larger, naked man grabbed Robin and pulled her to him. His erection pressed between her buttocks while he put the knife to her throat.

"You'll answer the door," Amy said to Frank. "If you say the wrong thing Vince will cut Robin's throat."

"What if it's the police?" Frank asked, urgently.

"Look through the peephole."

Frank went to the door and Amy followed. Vince held Robin tightly to him, licked her ear, rubbed his penis against her and pressed the tip of the knife harder into the flesh of her neck.

Frank looked through the peephole and said, "God, it's that detective . . ."

"Jones?" Amy asked, excitedly. This was too good. They would get to have some revenge on him, too.

"Yes."

"Open the door and get him inside."

"But—"

"Do it!" Amy hissed.

She waved at Vince, who pulled Robin into the kitchen. Amy moved so that she would be hidden behind the open door. Frank wondered what she expected to do against the detective without a weapon.

He took a deep breath and opened the door.

The door opened and Jones saw Frank Lobianco standing there in a bathrobe.

"What a relief," Jones said. "I tried calling but no one answered. Is Robin here?"

"Yes," Frank said. "We were, uh, busy."

Jones took that to mean they were having sex. A good sign. Maybe they were getting back together. He wondered if Robin had told Frank about the night with Vince and Amy. He hoped not. He didn't know if Frank would be able to get past it. He wasn't sure he would.

"I don't want to intrude—"

"Oh, that's, uh, all right," Frank said. "Why don't you come on in? We'll, uh, make some coffee."

He thought Frank seemed nervous. Maybe he had actually interrupted them . . .

"Come on," Frank said, "Robin will be glad to see you."

"Well, okay," Jones said, "maybe I could use the phone to call my partner."

"Sure . . ."

Frank backed away to allow Jones to enter. The detective had barely cleared the door when it slammed shut. He turned quickly and saw Amy Wheaton standing there, totally naked. He was shocked when she posed for him, hip shot, hands on hips.

"What do you think?" she asked.

"I've seen better," he said. The smile on her face slipped a bit. "Of course, I prefer women with tattoos . . ."

"Oh?" she said. She turned so that he could see her ass and looked at him over her shoulder. "Like this one?"

Bingo!

"That's the one," he said. "Mrs. Wheaton, you're under arrest."

"Is that a fact?"

"It is," he said. "Where's your husband?"

"He's in the kitchen," Frank said, "with Robin."

Suddenly, the situation became clear. Vince and Amy had come here with murder on their minds. As with the Brenda Telford killing, they intended to commit the murder naked. Since there was nowhere that Amy could be hiding a weapon he assumed that Vince had it in the kitchen with him and Robin.

"Come on out, Vince!" he called. "Time to clear all this up."

"You don't look surprised to see us, Detective," Amy said, as Vince came out of the kitchen with a frightened Robin clasped tightly to him. "Could it be you're smarter than I gave you credit for?"

"Nah," Jones said, "that couldn't be. Maybe I'm just luckier." After all, he thought, he wasn't smart enough to turn off his radio when he entered the building.

"And maybe not," Amy said. "All right, everyone's here and Robin has made her decision."

"She rejected you, huh?" Jones asked. "Not easy for people like you to take, is it? Like you were rejected by that woman in Omaha? You killed her boyfriend, though. I imagine the Omaha police would like to talk to the two of you about that."

Amy's smile froze and in a tight voice she said to him, "Let's start by relieving you of your gun."

Jones had to think fast and he came to a decision he hoped would not backfire on him.

"I don't think I can do that, Amy."

Robin made a sound and Jones could see that Vince had nicked her with the knife.

"That the same knife you used on Brenda Telford, Vince?"

"Don't answer him," Amy said, quickly. "He can't prove a thing."

"That's where you're wrong," Jones said. "You see, knife blades are like fingerprints. Our lab will match that one to the wounds on the body in no time. Also, I have a picture of you in the apartment."

"What?" Vince asked.

"He's lying," Amy said.

"Actually, Vince," he said, "we have a picture of your wife's delicious little ass, easily identifiable because of that perfect little rose tattoo."

"How'd he get a picture?" Vince asked Amy.

"I told you, he's lying," Amy said.

"And how's he know about Om—"

"Quiet, Vince," Amy said. "Don't say another word."

"The man you killed was holding a camera when you broke into the apartment, remember?" Jones asked them. "It fell to the floor and snapped off one picture. After you killed them you put the camera back on the shelf with all the others. That's where I found it."

"The camera—" Vince started.

"Shut up!" Amy snapped.

"The case cracked when it fell," Jones said. "I noticed it and you didn't, but then I'm a trained detective and you two are just a couple of degenerate killers. You're not even savvy enough to be Bonnie & Clyde."

"Where's this picture?" Amy asked.

"In my pocket."

"Show me."

Jones reached into his jacket pocket and took it out. He held it up so she would see it, but not so she could reach it.

"Give it to me," she said.

"Come and get it."

"Why? So you can grab me?" she asked. "Never mind. I'll take it off your dead body."

"Okay," Jones said, returning the photo to his pocket, "let's end this right now. I have a gun, you have a knife. You ever seen Sean Connery in the *Untouchables*?"

"What's he talking about?"

"I think," Frank said, "he means 'never take a knife to a gunfight'."

"Exactly."

He flipped his jacket back over the gun, feeling like an old west gunfighter. There was really no personal tension here. He was in no danger. He could get the gun out in plenty of time to keep these two from hurting him, and he could probably save Frank, as well.

The problem was going to be in keeping Vince from killing Robin.

THIRTY-EIGHT

He did the only thing he could.

"I can't do it."

"What?" Amy asked.

"I can't give you my gun," he said. "It's against regulations. I'll get in trouble."

"You'll get dead if you don't!" Vince snapped.

"Really, Vince?" Jones asked. "Are you going to kill me from there with that knife?"

"He'll kill her if you don't give me your gun," Amy said.

"For Chrissake," Frank pleaded, "give her your gun. He'll kill her."

"Frank," Jones said, "if I give her my gun they'll kill all three of us. If I don't—well, they'll kill Robin, but once Vince doesn't have her to hide behind, I'll shoot him." He looked at Amy. "Then I'll arrest you, Amy, and you'll end up in prison where a bunch of bull dykes will really appreciate your perfect little charms."

He didn't know what would alarm her more, the prospect of seeing her husband killed, or ending up in jail, so he thought he'd try them both. He was also hoping that his flip attitude would throw them off. However, Amy's face remained expressionless, which in itself was an accomplishment. At least he'd managed to wipe that arrogant look off her face.

"So we have a standoff," Frank said, hoping to convince Vince and Amy.

"Or there's another way." Jones took out his gun,

pointed it at Amy and cocked the hammer back. The sound seemed extra loud in the silence.

"Drop the knife, Vince," he said, "or I'll blow Amy's head off right in front of you."

"Y-you can't—" Vince said. "I love her."

"I know that," Jones said.

"Don't drop it, Vince," Amy said.

"But—"

"You heard what he said about me going to prison," she said. "I can't do that. I'd rather be dead. So you kill Robin, and let him kill me. That way I won't have to see you die."

Jones frowned. Had he outsmarted himself with the remark about prison dykes? Was she actually willing to die, instead?

He hadn't seen one in a while, but Amy Wheaton was turning out to be a tough broad.

Luckily, a lot tougher than her husband.

"No!" Vince said. "No, don't shoot."

"Vince!" Amy shouted. "Cut her throat."

"N-no, I can't . . ." Vince said, and dropped the knife.

No sooner had it hit the floor than Robin took one step away from him, pivoted and kicked him in the balls. If his erection had not already wilted it would have as he gagged and fell to his knees.

Robin turned then, strode up to Amy and punched her in the face. She hurt her hand but was very satisfied to see Amy's nose burst into a blossom of red.

Then she turned on Jones, who backed away a step.

"You bastard!" she shouted. "You were going to let him kill me."

"I knew he wouldn't," Jones lied. "Excuse me." He stepped past her and retrieved the knife.

Suddenly, it was as if she realized for the first time that

she was naked. She crossed one arm over her breasts—barely hiding them, he noticed—and the other hand went in front of her crotch.

"I'm going to go put something on," she said. "Am I right in assuming we're going to have company?"

"A lot of it," Jones said. "You better both get dressed. You'll have to come along, as well."

Robin turned to go down the hall to the bedroom, but Frank didn't move.

"You go first," he said, when she looked at him.

"All right," she said, and she knew what he was thinking. She wondered if they would ever be able to get past this.

"Frank," Jones said, just to give the man something to do, "slap these on Vince while I call for some assistance."

"With pleasure," Frank said, catching the cuffs.

Jones looked down at Amy, who had slumped to the floor, holding both hands to her bleeding nose. Her eyes, though, remained riveted on him, drilling into him with hatred.

"Guess your husband just wasn't as ready to die as you were, Amy," he said.

She just glared at him.

"By the way," he added, "that's a killer tattoo. It's going to be a big help in putting you away."

EPILOGUE

One Month Later . . .

"I needed someone to talk to," Robin told Jones when he arrived, "and I couldn't think of anyone else."

"That's okay," he said, sitting across from her. "My wife no longer thinks we're having an affair."

"Well," she said, "that's good. She probably doesn't like me any better, though."

Jones didn't respond.

They had lunch and talked and he gave her several scenarios of what might ultimately happen to the Wheatons, and how St. Louis and Omaha might end up fighting over them. But that wasn't really what she wanted to talk about. Eventually, she brought up the problem with Frank and asked him, as a married man, how he would feel in that situation?

"Robin," he said, "even that night, when you were all standing around naked—"

"Don't remind me."

"Well, I was hoping then that you hadn't told him, and wouldn't."

"I would have," she said. "I felt I had to, and would have if they hadn't done it. It was so much more hurtful coming from them."

"I don't know what I'd do in that situation," he said. "I mean . . . I'm married to a younger woman who has, well, an unusual job. She has a lot more opportunities than you would through your job. But I trust her, and if I found out that she had . . . done that to me, it would devastate me, simply because I never would have suspected."

"I think that's what Frank is feeling," she said. "I don't think it ever occurred to him that I would do something . . . like that. I know it never occurred to me, either."

"I guess all you can do is wait," he said, putting his big hand over hers. "Give him time."

"I know," she said. She took hold of his hand and squeezed it, her eyes shining with tears. "I miss Brenda so much. Normally, I'd talk to her about something like this."

"I'm flattered, then, that you called me," Jones said.

"I consider us friends, Jack."

"That's good," he said. "I need all the friends I can get."

"Your . . . situation at work hasn't improved?"

Actually, he was back on the charts catching cases on a regular basis. He didn't have a regular partner yet, but he'd been talking to Singleton about it and was leaving the decision up to him. But solving one case had not rid him of the stigma losing three partners had cast over him. It was going to take a little longer . . .

"I'm fine," he told her. "Really. So, what are you going to do?"

"I'll meet with Frank and see what he wants to do," she said. "I really think the decision is up to him."

"Let me know what happens."

"I will." She reached out and took his hands. "I can't thank you enough for everything."

"I did my job, Robin."

"And a little extra?" she asked.

"Yes," he said, with a smile, "and a little extra."

The next morning Frank called her at home and asked if he could meet with her. She suggested lunch or dinner, but he just said he wanted to see her. They agreed to meet at the base of the statue of St. Louis around noon, and here she was. Her heart was pounding almost as hard as it had been that night, with Vince's penis pressed against her naked butt and the knife held to her throat. Once he'd dropped the knife she'd been so incensed at all of them—Vince, Amy *and* Jones—that she wanted to lash out.

Now there was no one to lash out at. This was her own doing, and she could only wait . . .

She heard a car pull up and peered around the statue's base. She saw Frank's car and watched as he got out. His shoulders seemed slumped and she ducked back around the statue before she could see more. She didn't want to watch him walk, fearing she'd be able to predict what he was going to say.

"Hi," he said, coming around the base.

"Hello."

He stood next to her, looking out over the fountain.

"It's been a while," he said.

"Yes."

"I've been thinking."

"I know." She looked at him, at his profile. Wanted to reach out and touch him. "I'm scared, Frank."

"I was scared all those months, Robin," he said, "scared you'd never come back." He turned and looked at her. "I didn't think I could . . . get past what you did, but then I started thinking about that night, when Vince and Amy came to kill us. My God, they were going to kill us!"

"I know."

"I would have had to watch you die, or you me," he said, "whichever way they decided to go first." Now he reached out and took her hands. "The prospect of watching you die makes everything else pale by comparison. I . . . I want you to come home."

She stared at him, almost in disbelief. She'd almost convinced herself that he'd never be able to forgive her.

"I love you," he said.

She threw her arms around his neck and cried. It was several moments before she could say, "I love you, too, Frank."

"Will you come home?"

She stepped back and wiped her eyes and face with the palms of her hands.

"I—I'd have to give up my walk-in closet," she said. "I really love that thing."

He smiled and said, "So, we'll just move. We'll find a place to live where you can have a walk-in closet twice the size of the one you have now."

She smiled back, her first honest, relaxed smile in months and said, "Well, there's an offer a girl just can't turn down."

Jack Jones closed the door behind him and kicked off his shoes. He was tired. In the month since he'd captured "the Husband-and-Wife Stalker/Murderers," as the newspapers had christened them, nothing much had changed as far as the attitudes of his colleagues. The papers hadn't even mentioned him, saying only that Captain Phillips and "the detective assigned to the case, Ted Singleton," made statements.

At least Singleton had the decency to lower his eyes every time Jones walked into the room. Maybe that's what was keeping the man from making a decision about partnering with Jones. Well, whatever happened at least he was back doing real police work—for a while. And he wasn't seeing the department shrink anymore. He'd had about enough of her. At least Phillips had gone to bat for him in that regard.

"That you, hon?" Katy shouted from the kitchen.

"Yeah, it's me." He tried for chipper with his tone but could only manage desultory. At least he didn't sound suicidal.

"How was your day?" she called.

"It sucked."

"Well," she said, "come into the kitchen and I'll cheer you up."

She was cooking? She was not the greatest cook in the world, so maybe she just had a big bucket of KFC in there to cheer him up with.

"I hope you got plenty of breasts—" he was saying as he walked in, but he swallowed his words when he saw her and stopped in his tracks.

All she was wearing was an apron. She cocked her hip, raised an eyebrow at him and asked, "Is this enough breast for you?"

ABOUT THE AUTHOR

Brooklyn native Robert J. Randisi spent eight years as an NYPD administrative aide all the while pursuing his writing career at nights and on weekends. His job with the New York police gave him the opportunity to see the world of crime firsthand, thus lending both his stories and novels a real authenticity, which critics have always lauded him for.

In the early 1980s, Randisi left the police department to write full-time—and write he did. He became one of the most prolific of contemporary writers in the fields of both western and crime fiction. He has had over 350 books published since 1982.

He also found time to create the Private Eye Writers of America and to become the co-creator of *Mystery Scene*, the crime field's mystery magazine, and has edited more than a dozen prestigious anthologies.

But it is for his increasingly deft, polished and powerful crime fiction that Randisi will be best remembered. His first three Joe Keough novels established Randisi as one of the strongest and most unique voices in contemporary suspense fiction.

That same polish and power can be found in his collection of stories about his Brooklyn private eye Nick Delvecchio. The stories are spare, surprising and pack the same melancholy power as the two Delvecchio novels—*No Exit From Brooklyn* and *The Dead of Brooklyn*.

Robert currently lives in St. Louis and is the father of two sons.

The employees of Five Star hope you have enjoyed this book. All our books are made to last. Other Five Star books are available at your library, through selected bookstores, or directly from us.

For information about titles, please call:

(800) 223-1244

or visit our Web site at:

www.gale.com/fivestar

To share your comments, please write:

Publisher
Five Star
295 Kennedy Memorial Drive
Waterville, ME 04901